WHAT MR. MATTERO DID

ALSO BY

PRISCILLA CUMMINGS

Red Kayak

Saving Grace

A Face First

Autumn Journey

WHAT MR. MATTERO DID

Priscilla Cummings

DUTTON CHILDREN'S BOOKS

DUTTON CHILDREN'S BOOKS
A division of Penguin Young Readers Group
Published by the Penguin Group
Penguin Group (USA) Inc., 375 Hudson Street, New York, New York 10014, U.S.A.
Penguin Group (Canada), 90 Eglinton Avenue East, Suite 700, Toronto, Ontario, Canada M4P 2Y3
(a division of Pearson Penguin Canada Inc.)
Penguin Books Ltd, 80 Strand, London WC2R 0RL, England
Penguin Ireland, 25 St Stephen's Green, Dublin 2, Ireland (a division of Penguin Books Ltd)
Penguin Group (Australia), 250 Camberwell Road, Camberwell, Victoria 3124, Australia
(a division of Pearson Australia Group Pty Ltd)
Penguin Books India Pvt Ltd, 11 Community Centre, Panchsheel Park, New Delhi - 110 017, India
Penguin Group (NZ), Cnr Airborne and Rosedale Roads, Albany, Auckland 1310,
New Zealand (a division of Pearson New Zealand Ltd)
Penguin Books (South Africa) (Pty) Ltd, 24 Sturdee Avenue,
Rosebank, Johannesburg 2196, South Africa
Penguin Books Ltd, Registered Offices: 80 Strand, London WC2R 0RL, England

This book is a work of fiction. Names, characters, places, and incidents are either the product of the author's imagination or are used fictitiously, and any resemblance to actual persons, living or dead, business establishments, events, or locales is entirely coincidental.

LIBRARY OF CONGRESS CATALOGING–IN–PUBLICATION DATA
Cummings, Priscilla, date.
What Mr. Mattero did / by Priscilla Cummings.—1st ed.
p.   cm.
Summary: Three seventh-grade girls accuse their music teacher of having touched them
inappropriately and sexually.
ISBN 0-525-47621-0
[1. Music teachers—Fiction. 2. Teachers—Fiction. 3. Schools—Fiction. 4. Honesty—Fiction.
5. Sex crimes—Fiction. 6. Family life—Fiction.] I. Title: What Mister Mattero did. II. Title.
PZ7.C9149Wh 2005
[Fic]—dc22   2004028225

Published in the United States by Dutton Children's Books,
a division of Penguin Young Readers Group
345 Hudson Street, New York, New York 10014
www.penguin.com/youngreaders

Designed by Irene Vandervoort

Printed in USA   First Edition
10 9 8 7 6 5 4 3 2 1

"This above all: to thine own self be true . . ."

—WILLIAM SHAKESPEARE

① Claire

THIS WAS THE PLAN: second period, when we had earth science together, we would meet by the girls' bathroom and go straight to the office instead of class. We would say we needed to see the principal, Mrs. Fernandez, right away. And if the secretary said the principal was "busy" or "in a meeting," we would tell her it was an emergency. We would go together, the three of us—Jenna, Suzanne, and me. And if we got scared, like if one of us started to panic, we would reach out and hold hands, but we would not *break* down or *back* down.

Jenna would do the talking. There was never even a discussion about that. Only Jenna could lay out the facts without getting embarrassed the way Suzanne or I might. It's true. Jenna is, like, totally fearless. The third set of holes in her ears? She did them herself with a safety pin and an ice cube in her bathroom during winter break. Suzanne and I couldn't even watch, we were so freaked out. We jumped in the shower and pulled the door shut and sang "The Star-Spangled Banner" really, really loud.

But even Jenna needed to practice once—not piercing her ears but, you know, to be sure she could say certain things out loud. So we huddled that morning before school by the water fountain. I practically chewed off the thumbnail on my left hand, the only decent fingernail I had left, while Jenna, in a low voice, rehearsed what she would say. When she finished, when she pressed her lips together and looked at us with raised eyebrows, we nodded enthusiastically. We gave her a thumbs-up. We had a hundred percent confidence that Jenna could do it. That she could tell the principal what Mr. Mattero did to us in the music room.

I'm telling you, for two days we agonized over it. Should we say something? Should we just drop hints? And for two days, we had argued only once—when Suzanne said she worried what the other kids would think. "I mean, what if they look at us like we're whatchamacallit—weird or something."

I had frowned at her—I remember that—because I didn't know what she was getting at. Like, did she mean *victims*? Was she afraid kids would think we were victims? And so what if they did? What was wrong with that? Or did she mean something else, like did we do something to egg him on? I didn't know the word I was looking for then, but I know it now: *provoke*. Was she worried that kids would think we did something to *provoke* Mr. Mattero?

Jenna was just as confused as me. She had screwed up her face and leaned toward Suzanne. "What did you say?" She was already turned around on the bus seat in front of us and was sitting on her knees. She did that so we three could talk together, but it was incredibly noisy on the ride home after school. Sometimes, honestly, you have to get right in someone's face or practically shout to be heard.

"Weird! They'll think we're weird!" Suzanne repeated, very distinct and very loud, because you could tell she was a little bit angry, too.

Jenna laughed. She popped her gum. "Halfa them think we're weird anyway! So who cares?" Ouch. I think that hurt Suzanne. I know it hurt me. I mean, I never wanted kids to think I was weird or anything. Anyway, we're sort of getting off the subject here because what was far more important at the moment was that I, for one, did not think we should be *laughing* or *hollering* about any of this. "You guys! Shhhhhhh!" I warned, holding a finger to my lips.

Suzanne scooted forward and continued anyway, talking in that tiny little pleading voice of hers. Whiny, that's what Jenna calls it. Her whiny voice: "I was just thinking that maybe we shouldn't say anything."

Jenna's intense eyes locked onto Suzanne's. "Look at me and tell me that you want to be in Mattero's music class the rest of the year."

Suzanne looked down at her hands.

"Do you want to have to look at his ugly face every single day for the rest of the semester?" Jenna persisted.

Suzanne trembled, a little like my mother's cell phone on the vibrate mode. I mean, you could actually see her shake.

"Do you?" Jenna demanded.

Timidly, Suzanne shook her head in tiny back-and-forth motions.

"No. No! Of course you don't! Then we have to speak up, Suzanne. We don't have a choice. Claire and me, we'll go in there without you if we have to." She glared at me. "Won't we, Claire?"

That's when I first started biting the rest of that good thumb-nail off. And after all those weeks of leaving my nails alone! Reluctantly, I nodded, agreeing with Jenna.

Suzanne was sucking on her bottom lip, the way she does. I told her she ought to stop it. Not that *I* care—we go back a long ways, Suzanne and me, all the way back to kindergarten—so I'm not the one who's gonna give her grief. But she really ought to give up the lip thing 'cause the kids in this middle school are gonna call her a frickin' baby if she keeps it up.

"Hey," I said, poking Suzanne's shoulder. When she looked up, I encouraged her with a teensy smile because I knew Jenna was watching.

"Okay, *okay.*" Suzanne gave up. She widened her eyes. "Whatever."

"Good!" Jenna pronounced like that was that, and with a

sniff, too, because she was on the brink of a cold. "We're best friends, remember?"

True. Now *that* was true. We were best friends. We had been best friends since the beginning of seventh grade—so, for what? Seven months? We were in almost all the same classes. We were online or on the phone with each other after school. And practically every Friday we had a sleepover, rotating to our different houses, but mostly to mine and Suzanne's because Jenna's mother was away so much.

There is no question that Jenna and Suzanne were the two best friends I ever had, although anybody who didn't know us might wonder what in the world we three had in common. I mean, Jenna's so blonde and has perfect skin and everything, while Suzanne and I are so—I don't know, ordinary. Okay, maybe that's cruel to say because once Suzanne gets her braces off—and when her skin clears up, she'll be incredibly cute. She looks good in clothes even if she thinks she's too fat. She is *not* fat! And her hair—wow—too much, too curly, too red, she says—but everyone else, including me, thinks it's really pretty.

For sure, I'm the one who's no raging beauty. Jenna says I just need to let my bangs and layers grow out. She says I'm really smart and that I have a classic Roman nose and awesome brown eyes and not everyone tans, just look at Suzanne, and wait till I'm older—I can use that dermabrasion stuff to get the freckles off. Oh yeah, and she says that lots of girls wish they

were as skinny as me. She swears she's not kidding, but sometimes she just says stuff, you know?

Jenna was reaching out her hand to me on the bus while all
that stuff went through my mind. "Claire, peachy, can I borrow
your lip gloss? That sparkly one?"

"Oh yeah, sure." I hauled up my backpack from the floor and
unzipped the little pocket on the side where I kept the gum
and Tic Tacs that warded off my constant hunger, a fistful of
makeup, and change for the soda machine. When I found what
she wanted, Snow Kiss, I placed it in her waiting palm.

"Thanks," she said. She popped her gum again. "You're sweet."

While Jenna dipped her pinkie in the lip-gloss pot, I brushed
the wispy hair ends out of my eyes and glanced at Suzanne
again. The way she sat, slouched back into the seat, it didn't
look like she was convinced. And I have to admit, I was a little
worried myself—but more about my mom than about what the
other kids would say. I never said so to Jenna, though, because
I didn't want her to think I was weak.

Later, after we got home that day, Suzanne and Jenna IM'd
each other back and forth like crazy on their computers so that
by the next morning Suzanne was gung ho in total agreement
that we would tell the principal. I wasn't part of their online
conversation because our family computer is in the kitchen,
facing the island where my mother puts the salad and everything together. I didn't think I could take the chance of anyone
looking over my shoulder.

I don't know. Maybe I should have tapped away on that keyboard anyway and let my mother find out. See, I've always thought we should have told our mothers first. "Let *them* march into Mrs. Fernandez's office," I had suggested to Jenna the very first time we ever talked about it. "Our moms are going to find out anyhow."

"Claire, this is something we have to do ourselves," Jenna had argued. "Besides, my mom's not home this week."

Nothing new. Jenna's mom is a flight attendant and she's away a lot. Paris one week. Honolulu the next. No wonder it was so easy to lose track of her. I used to think she was such a good mother, too. She was always bringing Jenna stuff: cute little fish earrings, flashy pareos, cool bathing suits—and those fancy macadamia nuts. She used to give us each a jar every time she flew in from Hawaii. Ha! I ought to tell her sometime how I used to eat maybe one nut and chuck the rest in the backyard for the squirrels because they're like two hundred calories for about five of them.

Yeah, yeah, yeah. So there's a part of me that's a little bit mean, too. But you know what? If you took a good look at my life sometime, you'd see why. Still, it just kills me to think about how I envied Jenna because of her mom. I mean, my mother seemed sooooo incredibly boring next to hers. All my mom did every day was stay home, working on her food list, doing stacks of laundry, fawning and fretting over my little brother and sister—mostly my brother—and asking me annoying questions like: "Claire, have you done your homework yet?" "Claire, did you pick up your room?" "Claire, is that all you're going to eat?"

Sheesh.

But now that I think of it, Jenna's mom should have been a little bit more like *mine*. Hey! And maybe none of this would have happened. Who knows?

"Look, Jenna, we can wait until your mom gets back," I had suggested, in my most kindest, most sane voice.

Jenna grew quiet when I said that. I know Jenna missed her mom. You could always tell when her mother was flying. (I guess I should put that in quotes or something—the word "flying.")

Suddenly Jenna pulled the elastic out of her ponytail and shook back her long hair. "I'm thinking of getting more highlights this week. You wanna come with me?"

I stared at her. If arrows could have come out of my eyeballs, they would have.

"Claire, come on, you should come with me—"

"Jenna!" I hated it when she didn't finish a conversation. "I said maybe we should wait till your mom gets back."

"No!" Jenna had shot back.

It sort of shocked me, her tone. It had a nasty edge to it. I pulled back.

Jenna softened her voice. "Look, we already talked about that." And instantly, like she pressed a button or something, her eyes got all red and watery, too, like she was going to cry.

"Remember?" Jenna asked. "We all agreed—we have to tell someone *now*."

What is it about her? You look at Jenna and you think, here is a girl who has everything going for her, but somehow she can make you feel sorry for her like nobody I have ever known in my entire life. So I may have hesitated and rolled my eyes. Maybe I even cussed at her under my breath. But I went along with it. At that point I committed.

I could kick myself, though—*real hard*. And I still say that if our mothers had all known first, it might have played out different. With a little more warning, Suzanne's mother might not have gotten so off-the-wall hysterical, and for sure, Jenna's father wouldn't have come barreling into school the way he did, swinging his fists. God, that was awful. I just can't believe it. It got everything—*everything* started off on the absolute wrong foot!

(2) Melody

I DIDN'T KNOW any of the seventh-grade girls who marched into the principal's office that day. We have a fairly large middle school—hundreds of kids—and even in my eighth-grade class I didn't know everyone. Up until the day when my life collided with Claire's, I had no idea who she was. Same for the redhead, Suzanne. I did recognize one of the girls, the one named Jenna. But I couldn't figure out *how* I knew her until one day weeks later when we passed each other outside the police detective's office.

Odd how some of the most profound events of your life—things that can change you as a person forever—happen when you least expect it. At the exact moment those girls walked into the principal's office at Oakdale Middle School and started everything, I was alone in the music room arranging the chairs for band practice.

I had a study hall that period, and I knew the music room was a mess. It was not a big deal. I was in the music room a lot when I had extra time: organizing music, stacking and unstacking the chairs, wiping the blackboard, clearing Diet Coke cans off the teacher's desk, picking up trash. I didn't do it because I love music or for extra credit. I did it because I wanted to do it—and because Mr. Mattero is my father.

Dad is very particular about the seating arrangement for band, so I did it according to his plan, plus I was careful to count, giving every two chairs a shared music stand because we didn't have enough for everyone. Well, all except for Sasha and Orlando, who were, respectively, our sole cello and trumpet players and needed their own music.

I didn't mind helping my father. Organization is not his strong point (an understatement), and Dad was very appreciative. Besides, while I pushed chairs around and unfolded the metal stands, I was simultaneously rhyming in my head and trying to find a phrase that rhymed with "drops of water": *playful otter . . . springtime squatter.* I wanted to be a writer—a poet, actually—and my best friend, Annie, and I were both writing something for the spring edition of *Wings*, our school literary magazine.

Just when I had the last chair in place, my father walked into the room holding a tall stack of CDs in his hands and using his chin to keep the pile stable. "Hey, Mel," he said, taking small but quick steps toward his desk.

I was surprised to see him. "I thought you had a teachers' meeting?"

"I did." He bent over and tried to settle the CDs on his desk, but the stack was so high it started to topple over, and we both rushed to stop it.

A loud clatter shattered the quiet. Throwing open my arms, I stopped about half a dozen from careening off the side of his desk.

"Good catch!" I exclaimed when Dad caught one an inch from the floor.

"Close indeed!" he agreed.

We both laughed. Dad straightened his keyboard tie, a birthday present from me, while I pushed my eyeglasses back up on my nose. Then I flipped my long braid back over my shoulder, and together, Dad and I restacked the CDs.

"Thanks, Mel," he said. "Hey, and thanks for setting up the chairs."

I nodded a welcome and pointed. "I organized the music, too. See?"

My father glanced at the neat piles of sheet music on his desk. "Great," he said. "Perfect. But could you do me one more favor before you leave?"

"Sure."

"Would you haul out that small viola from the storage room and rosin up the bow? I've got a sixth-grader, Lee somebody, who wants to try it."

Frowning, I crossed my arms. "Dad, you gave the little viola to Maura Shannahan."

At first, my father's face went blank—then it sagged with disappointment.

I stared at him. "Don't you remember? You gave it to her a week ago. She's already broken the A string! I had to put a new one on for her yesterday in band."

"Yeah, you're right," Dad said. He put a hand up to his forehead and rubbed it slowly, the way he does when he's thinking. Then he looked at me and winked. "Think I can talk her into a clarinet?"

I couldn't help but grin. "Probably," I said, but I was sure he could because my father is amazing when it comes to convincing kids to try new things. If he wasn't, we wouldn't have a middle-school band *or* an orchestra!

Dad rolled his shirtsleeves up and was getting back to work when the intercom came on. The light blinked, and the school secretary's loud, nasal voice accosted us: *"Mr. Mattero?"*

I turned and walked away, pulling my braid over my shoulder and twisting the end of it (a habit when I'm composing). I went back to writing that poem in my head, wondering if maybe *melting snow, things will grow* had more possibilities than *water, otter,* or *squatter.*

But when I think back on that moment—because Dad got called down to the office a minute later—I glimpse a snapshot of my father's face, and I can see all over again how upset he was, knowing he'd have to disappoint little Lee somebody who had wanted to try the viola. And I think of how my dad hated to squelch anyone's enthusiasm for music because he was really dedicated. That was the one true thing I have always known for sure: that my dad loved teaching music to kids. For twenty-two years, he taught music, half of those years at Oakdale Middle School.

My father thought everyone in the world needed to master at least one musical instrument while they were young: "It teaches self-discipline and creative thinking," he would tell you, would *beg* you to understand. "It builds self-confidence!" He went crazy when the school board threatened to cut music out of the middle-school budget to save money. "This would be a tragic mistake," he was quoted in the local newspaper. The clipping is still on our refrigerator. "Music and art are the building blocks that make people and our society a vibrant and viable world!"

Of course everyone in my family played an instrument—or two or three. (Even if you didn't really want to, I should add.) My older sister, away at college in Indiana where she is majoring in music and education, is a piano and flute virtuoso. Not to mention the fact that my sister composes some of her own pieces. She's a regular little Mozart in training. Every year in high school she was selected for All State Orchestra, and her goal is to be a music teacher—like my dad! Believe me, she is a very hard act to follow.

My brother, too, could be in the teenage music hall of fame. Not only does he play drums and guitar (for the rock band he organized in the sixth grade), but he's terrific on the saxo-phone, too. And he has the best ear of all of us when it comes to picking out a new tune. Don't be looking for him on the music circuit though. My brother, a sophomore in high school, is also the second-string quarterback for the Wallinsburg Cougars. His dream is not only to come from behind and lead an eighty-yard drive to win a playoff game against rival Rockville High School, but to hustle and make a million dollars as a professional football player for the Washington Redskins.

Still, it's music, music, music in our house. And just look at our names! My sister in college is Song. My brother is Cade, which is short for Cadence (the harmonic ending in a piece of music). There's me—Melody. (Did I forget to credit myself with the viola?) Even our cat is named Harmony.

I know, *I know*. It's all a bit much. But please don't compare us to the Brady Bunch because we're not dumb like that. It's just my parents' style, that's all. Underneath it all, they're really nice, really smart people. My mother, Mary, runs a plant nursery and plays flute in the community orchestra. She let me repaint my entire room lavender last summer, and she's hired someone to rebuild her old computer from work so that she can give it to me and I can have my own. My mother is the glue that holds our family together. And she stood by my father the entire time. She is still standing by him. I guess I should add that, too.

My father, Frederick Mattero (everyone calls him Fred)—well, up until this all happened, he was just a normal person. And he has been a great dad. I will never forget how he coached my soccer team in fourth grade, even though he didn't know anything about soccer. And how my dad—every summer since I was eight—has taken just me on a fishing trip down the Rappahannock River in Virginia and doesn't even care if I don't fish. While he casts around and reels in dinner, I sit on these flat rocks in the river and write poems. Then, while we're sitting by the campfire, I read him the poems I wrote, and he actually listens and he always has something meaningful, something insightful, to say about them.

But there are a kazillion little things my dad does—my dad *did*—for lots of people, not just me, that made him so special. I mean, his blueberry pancakes on Sunday morning, his turkey tacos, his sense of humor, all the help he gave Cade's band (even filling in one night when the drummer got sick), and the way my dad always knows the right thing to do. Gosh, and all the houses he's fixed up with the Habitat for Humanity people at church—and the kitchen with all the new cabinets that he renovated for my mom.

Sometimes, it doesn't make any sense that this has happened.

"Think I can talk her into a clarinet?"

"Probably."

It keeps coming back to me—the last conversation Dad and I had before the weight of the world was upon him—and me—and my family.

After the intercom came on and Dad got called down to the office, everything changed.

"Mr. Mattero, can you come down to the office right away? Mrs. Fernandez needs to talk to you."

Dad pushed a clarinet case against the wall with his foot and left, mumbling that he'd probably forgotten to get his homeroom lunch count in on time again and how Mrs. Fernandez shouldn't be wasting his time with stuff like that. I had finished setting up the chairs and then returned to study hall with my journal to work on a poem about spring that I never finished.

I don't know. It's hard to describe, but I'm different now. And it's not just the poetry I never write anymore or what happened to my best friend, Annie, and me. It has more to do with how I see my father, how we all see my father, and where we go from here.

It's confusing sometimes. Because up until the day Dad was accused by those seventh-graders, I figured my father's greatest weakness was just in being a little forgetful and disorganized. But over the next few months, I would come to know many things, good and bad, about my dad. Things that I might otherwise have never known.

And I can say the same about myself.

③ Claire

"YOU WAIT—THEY WILL GO FREAKING BALLISTIC!"

That was Jenna saying that—all the way down the hall to the school office. All the way grabbing my wrist and predicting—like she almost *enjoyed* this—what was going to happen when we three walked in.

But a lot of stuff goes down in middle school every day, and we hadn't counted on walking into another crisis when we went to report ours.

Everyone in the office that morning was busy—the secretary with a deliveryman and teachers walking in and out getting their mail out of their little boxes. So we stood at the counter and looked toward where the yelling was coming from: Mrs. Fernandez's office. The door was not closed all the way, so I was able to see part of a denim jacket and an ugly little rattail, and I knew right off who it was.

"Jason," I whispered to Jenna. "Jason's in there."

"Jason?"

Like how many Jasons did she know? Because I could only think of one. "Jason *Hershel*," I told her.

And we all nodded—you know, "aha!"—on account of we knew why he was in there. It was for bringing those firecrackers on our bus that morning.

Actually, if you want to know the truth, I'm glad he got hauled in. I don't much like Jason. He still calls me "Tubs" even after all the weight I've lost. But more than that, those firecrackers sounded just like a gun going off, and that's not funny. We all dove down in our seats and little Madeline Ott cut her lip hitting the floor and was bleeding all over the place, including on my new sandals when I went over to help her up. When the bus pulled over, we all saw Jason laughing his head off. But in a weird kind of way that was a relief. Because then we all knew it was just Jason and not like real bullets flying around in there.

Jason is so over the top. I remember in first grade how he and his older brother rented out *Playboy* magazines on the bus. For a quarter you got to look at one for, like, five minutes before Jason grabbed it back and hid it in his backpack. Not that I ever paid to look at one, but I did catch a glimpse.

You know, I always wondered what those girls got paid for posing in those *Playboy* pictures. I mean, exposing their privates like that, did they like get paid a lot? I'll tell you this. Those pictures were *provocative*. I know that word now, and I am here to tell you that no matter what those parents said, none of us could ever be called *provocative* compared with those *Playboy* pictures!

Anyway, a narrow view is all I had of Jason. Enough to see his dumb head nodding slowly, like on automatic. "Yes, ma'am . . . yes, ma'am." Even Jason would not want to take on Mrs. Fernandez or give her any crap because she is one tough, bull moose of a woman. I think she could've picked up Jason with one hand and stuffed him in her wastebasket if she had wanted. When the yelling was over, Jason shuffled out with Mrs. Fernandez right on his heels.

"Remember, that's a warning, Jason," Mrs. Fernandez called after him.

I started getting cold feet then—and butterflies in my stomach—seeing Mrs. Fernandez all red-faced and worked up after yelling at Jason. But Jenna didn't wait for her to cool down.

"Mrs. Fernandez!" she called out.

The principal turned her head toward us.

"We need to talk to you," Jenna said quickly. "Suzanne and Claire and me."

I swallowed hard, and Suzanne shot me a desperate look.

Jenna sucked in her breath. "Something's happened, and we need to report it."

Mrs. Fernandez frowned and came over. When she stood on the other side of the counter from us, Suzanne and I scooted close together.

Jenna raced on. "Something happened in the music room,

Mrs. Fernandez. A teacher did something that we don't feel very good about . . ."

Mrs. Fernandez sighed. You could tell she did not want to deal with us. "Girls, if you're having a problem in class, then we need to arrange a parent-teacher conference—"

"No!" Jenna stopped her. "We need to tell you because we're pretty sure it was abuse. We think it was sexual abuse."

Instantly, and I mean *instantly*, the office became silent. The secretary stopped keyboarding. The receptionist put a hand over the mouthpiece of her phone. Even the FedEx man froze with a package in his hand. For a minute there, we must have looked like we were in a commercial or something. At least that's how it felt. Like it wasn't real somehow. Like we were outside ourselves, watching it.

At first Mrs. Fernandez seemed confused. But then she motioned for us to come around the counter—and she separated us! "You in here, in my office," she said to Jenna as she took her by the arm.

We three glanced at one another, our eyes saying what we could not say out loud: *Remember everything. Be strong. We're best friends.*

After Jenna disappeared behind the office door, Mrs. Fernandez pointed her index finger at the room next door, the office of our assistant principal, and told Suzanne to go in there. But Suzanne just stared at her, like she was paralyzed. Then she started doing her lip-sucking thing, and there was a terrible, awkward moment when neither one of them moved. Mrs. Fernandez stood with her finger pointing and her gold charm bracelet dangling off her beefy wrist until Suzanne finally obeyed.

"And *you*," Mrs. Fernandez said, motioning to me. She put a hand on my shoulder and looked around. Mrs. Sidley, my English teacher, was coming toward us with a bunch of papers in her hands. The principal asked her, "Could you please escort this young lady down to the guidance office?"

Mrs. Sidley's surprised eyes caught mine. "Certainly," she said.

I followed my English teacher's big butt down a narrow hallway in the back of the office to the guidance counselor's office and sat down on a hard plastic chair. The room didn't have a real window in it, but the guidance counselor had made a fake one so it looked like it did. She put curtains up around a poster of a pretty-phony-looking mountain scene from Switzerland or someplace. Someplace with chalet houses. I mean, who is she kidding? We know that there is not a snow-capped mountain with chalets and cows grazing in the meadow across the street from Oakdale Middle School. There's no *oak* and there's no *dale* either. Just a trashy two-lane highway with a traffic light in front of the school driveway that blinks yellow all the time. And on the other side is a dry cleaner's run by a Chinese family and Frank's Auto Body Shop, where my cousin, Herky, works.

EAGLES SOAR. YOU CAN TOO, another poster shouted. Boy, I

wished I was an eagle and could've soared right out of there.

Nervous, my eyes flicked to yet another poster, all fancy writing: *To thine own self be true . . . —William Shakespeare.*

I wondered what that meant, that Shakespeare quote. I thought about it while I was waiting on the hard chair to tell Mrs. Fernandez what Mr. Mattero did. And I thought I had that quote figured out, that it meant to always be the kind of person on the outside that you were on the inside. Or vice versa. In other words, to not be a big fat hypocrite or anything.

And *that* made me think back to when I was new in middle school. To sixth grade, how I was myself—and how that didn't do me a lick of good because nobody liked me. I was a little bit chunky then—that was before my diet—and all my old friends from fifth grade, suddenly they were wearing really sexy clothes all the time—like tight jeans and crop tops—and talking to boys online after school and planning to hook up at the movies, and I didn't want to do that stuff. (Of course, it's not like I turned them down because they never even called me anymore.)

Suzanne was the only friend who stayed a friend in sixth grade. Those girls didn't much like Suzanne either, but I don't know why. Because of her asthma? Because she has to use an inhaler and she can't run and do all the things we do in gym? Because she's shy? Because of her bad skin? What? I don't know. But we stuck together. We ate lunch together every day, peanut butter and jelly sandwiches, Cheetos, Oreos—a lot of junk food, come to think of it. Then, after school, after Suzanne and me got off the bus, we'd hang out at her house or my house and do our homework together. We played basketball Wednesday nights at the rec center, and on weekends we hooked up and went to the mall, even if it was just to visit the puppies in the pet store or squirt stuff on each other at Bath & Body Works.

Still, it was a lonely year. At school all the time we had to listen to those other girls—girls who used to be our friends—whispering and giggling about their sleepovers and boys they liked and stuff like that. I didn't like sixth grade, and I didn't much like myself either. I stopped eating in sixth grade.

The next year, when school started, Suzanne and me and some other kids in our neighborhood got transferred to a different school because of overcrowding. I was glad, but it didn't make any difference, because the cool girls at Oakdale ignored us, too—even though I had lost all that weight over the summer. Then, pretty soon after school started, Jenna moved into our neighborhood and showed up on our bus. She was so hot, I remember thinking how Jenna could pick any of the popular girls at Oakdale and be, like, friends immediately. But she didn't. She decided she didn't like the popular girls at our new school. She said they were sluts. She picked us—Suzanne and me—instead. I couldn't believe it. I mean, who would have thought that could happen?

A couple of minutes passed while I was thinking back on

how we became friends. I looked at the clock and wondered what we were missing in earth science. We were doing the chapter on weather, on wind and evaporation and stuff. Would the teacher notice we weren't there?

I was tired of reading posters on the wall, but there wasn't anything else to do. One of them said that getting respect starts with respecting yourself. I swung my head around to look out the door. Well, so far, Mrs. Fernandez hadn't shown much respect for any of us. We weren't bad kids like Jason Hershel, who brought firecrackers on the bus that could actually hurt someone. Besides, didn't she care about what we said? What one of her teachers did? Didn't she know what kind of courage it took for us to just walk in her office?

Mrs. Sidley, who had been very quiet, peeked back in looking a little sorry for me. "Claire, what happened?" she finally asked, stepping into the doorway.

I have always liked Mrs. Sidley. Even if she does fix her hair like someone out of the fifties, I like the books we read in her class, and I got halfway decent grades from her. I opened my mouth to explain, but the words wouldn't rise up. Suddenly she was shaking her head, saying, "No, no, don't. I'm probably not supposed to ask."

So I closed my mouth, and while Mrs. Sidley kept watch, I sat there on that chair, hugging my backpack, chewing on what was left of my poor, torn-up fingernail, and feeling myself break out into little beads of sweat.

Finally, Mrs. Fernandez came in. Mrs. Sidley gave me a "good luck" look with a lift of her eyebrows and left. The principal closed the door.

"All right," she began, sighing and taking a hard look at me. "What's *your* name?" She sounded tired.

"Claire," I told her. "Claire Montague."

"Claire Montague," she repeated. I guess because she didn't know me. "You're new this year, Claire? Seventh grade?"

"Yes, ma'am. I'm new because of the districting."

"You mean *re*districting," she corrected me. "You got moved here from Herald Heights?"

I nodded.

Mrs. Fernandez started to shake her head, and I wondered if she thought that maybe we wanted to cause trouble because we were unhappy about the move.

"I like this school," I quickly told her. "It's a whole lot better than my old one. At Herald Heights there is, like, a fight every day. You can't even take a regular backpack to that school—it has to be a clear one, you know? So they can see through to what you have in there, like a knife or something."

Mrs. Fernandez did not react to that.

"Claire," she continued, "often there are many sides to an incident."

Why was she calling it an incident? Didn't she believe Jenna?

She handed me some lined notebook paper and said very slowly, "I want you to write me a letter. Take your time and tell me everything that happened, okay? What led up to it and all the details you can remember."

I was surprised because I had thought we'd talk about it, that she would ask me some questions.

"Do you understand?" she asked.

I told her I did.

"All right then," she said. "Go ahead. Take your time." And she walked out. Just like that.

I was surprised, yes. But I was also relieved that I didn't have to talk to her about it. At that point, I just wanted to write it all down quickly and get out of there—maybe even fake a stomachache so I could go home.

After moving a couple books on the guidance counselor's desk so I had a flat space to write on, I smoothed out the paper. *Dear Mrs. Fernandez,* I wrote at the top in my neatest cursive.

We had notes—Jenna, Suzanne, and I—printed on pieces of bright pink Post-its that we'd stuffed into our jeans pockets. But I didn't need to look at those notes because I knew everything by heart.

I began to write.

④ Melody

THE RUMORS ABOUT MY DAD STARTED FAST. I eat during the last lunch on Wednesday, all the eighth-graders do, and by then I'd already been warned something had happened and that my father was involved. But I also knew he could be pretty outspoken, so I didn't think much about it. I figured Dad had an argument with Mrs. Fernandez about why school wasn't paying the instrument-repair bill on time. He'd been complaining about it at breakfast.

Then, on my way to class after lunch, my best friend, Annie, stopped me in the hallway and pulled me by my shirtsleeve into the girls' room. "Melody," she said, breathlessly, "your dad's in big trouble."

"What are you talking about?"

"Two kids I know . . . they were in the office . . . they heard your dad yelling at Mrs. Fernandez . . . I mean *really yelling—*"

"Annie—"

"No!" she stopped me. She took a breath. "Somebody else's

father—I don't know who—he tried to take a punch at your dad."

"What?"

"One of the teachers had to grab that guy and hold him back!"

"Annie, what in the world are you talking about?"

"It's what those kids told me!"

I grinned at her because Annie is so melodramatic. "Come on. You know Dad. He's always arguing with Mrs. Fernandez."

Annie's mouth made a tight line. You could tell she was disappointed in my reaction.

"Come on, we need to go," I told her, glancing at my watch. "We're going to be late."

Annie licked her lips, studying me. "All right," she agreed. "But promise me, Mellie, *promise*—if something happened, you'll call me right after school."

I chuckled. I actually chuckled! "I *promise*," I told her, which seemed so silly because we call each other anyway.

We came out of the bathroom, and I watched Annie walk down the hallway with all the key rings jangling off her backpack. Then I shrugged it off and went to gym.

In the locker room, which is too warm, smells like stinky feet, and is full of chaos with all of us rushing to change at once, I sat down on a bench between lockers. Right when I pulled my shoes off I heard my name called.

"Melody! Melody Mattero!" our gym teacher, Mrs. Anderson, sang out over the noise.

Some of the girls held clothes up to their fronts or quickly stepped into their gym shorts because suddenly Mrs. Anderson was right there in the door to our locker room.

I walked in my Peds over to where she stood and—it seemed so strange—Mrs. Anderson told me I had been chosen to participate in some sort of a survey. She told me I had to go down to the office and answer some questions. "Others will be asked to participate, too," she announced loudly to everybody who was staring. "You're excused, Melody. Go ahead."

I *still* didn't think it was anything unusual. I was in SGA (the student government association), and we were always getting asked to do extra things, like organize a food drive or decorate for the dance and plan refreshments. I figured it was SGA-related. And honestly, I did not mind missing gym because we were playing lacrosse and I'm not very good at flinging that hard little ball.

After putting my shoes back on, I picked up my books and went down to the office. No sign of my dad yelling at Mrs. Fernandez or getting punched out by someone's father. No police. *See?* I grinned, thinking I'd tell Annie: *"You were being melodramatic again."*

Mrs. Fernandez met me and said to come on back to the guidance counselor's office. Okay, I did think it was odd that the principal was escorting me. She was quiet, too, while we walked down the little hallway behind the main office. Usually, she asks about my sister, Song, or my brother, Cade—she really liked Cade. But she didn't chitchat at all.

In the guidance counselor's office, two people were waiting.

"Melody, this is Mr. Daniels and this is Miss Weatherall," Mrs. Fernandez said. "They would like to ask you a few questions. They're doing a survey, to make sure kids in school are safe."

I said hi to Mr. Daniels and Miss Weatherall. They seemed like nice people. Mr. Daniels shook my hand and pulled out a chair for me. He was young and fairly handsome, I thought, a little like Pierce Brosnan, with dark hair and a killer smile. "I hope you don't mind," he said. "We won't be long."

I cleared my throat. "No, no. It's fine."

Miss Weatherall had a bit of an odd look to her. She had mountains of frizzy hair, some of which she pulled back into a clip. And she wore an old-fashioned outfit, a long brown peasant skirt and a bulky brown sweater to match, but she was pleasant. She extended her hand as well. "It's a pleasure to meet you," she greeted me.

Miss Weatherall assured me their visit was routine. "We just want to ask you a few questions. We'll be talking to other kids, too."

See? When she said they would be talking to other kids, too, it *did* reassure me. Even then I didn't think it had anything to do with my father. It certainly never crossed my mind that Mr.

Daniels was a police detective with a gun hidden at his side and a badge tucked into his pocket!

"Have a seat," Mr. Daniels offered, gesturing to the chair he'd pulled out from a small round table. I sat down and adjusted my glasses. Mr. Daniels and Miss Weatherall sat opposite me. Miss Weatherall pulled out a small notebook and immediately started writing.

"So Melody," Mr. Daniels said, folding his hands on the tabletop, "what is your last name?"

"Mattero. M–a–t–t–e–r–o." I spelled it for him because some people have a hard time with my name. They get the *a*'s and the *e*'s transposed.

"Melody Mattero," he repeated. "And when is your birthday?"

"January 25," I said. "I'm fourteen."

"And you're in the eighth grade, is that correct?"

"Yes, that's right."

"Can you tell me a little bit about yourself?"

I must have looked a little confused.

"Brothers? Sisters? Who's at home?"

"Oh. Well, I have a sister in college. Out in Indiana. And a brother who's a junior at the high school. We live with my parents. At 138 Bellevue Avenue."

"What classes are you taking this year, Melody?"

"I'm in honors English," I said. "Then I have honors lit. That's literature. Then honors Spanish, honors social studies, honors algebra, health, and music."

"Whoa, that's quite a load!" Mr. Daniels noted. He seemed really impressed.

It *was* quite a load. Some nights I spent about five hours on homework. But I was doing okay, and my parents were really proud.

"How are your grades?" he asked. Miss Weatherall wasn't doing any of the asking, but she was writing really fast.

"All A's except for algebra," I told him. "Math is my downfall."

Mr. Daniels laughed. "Good ole algebra. I wasn't good at it either."

A pause. I smiled a little and looked back at him. I wondered if he had a list somewhere, or if he had just memorized all the questions he had to ask.

"What's your favorite subject?" he asked.

"English," I answered instantly. "I love reading. I love writing. I write poetry all the time."

"You do?"

I nodded eagerly. "I wrote a poem that was in our literary magazine last fall. I'm writing another one for the spring issue."

"That's fantastic. What was the name of your poem?" Mr. Daniels asked.

I hesitated because I didn't like to *talk* about my poems. I would rather people just read them.

Miss Weatherall stopped writing. "Does it have a title?" she repeated, waiting with her pen poised.

I felt my cheeks grow warm because my poems were per-

sonal, and I was a little self-conscious. "It's called 'The Secret,'"
I said.

The dark eyebrows on Mr. Daniels sprang up, and I caught
the look he exchanged with Miss Weatherall. He opened one
hand. "How does it go?" he asked. "What are the first couple
lines?"

"We'd love to hear some of it," Miss Weatherall added.

As I looked from one of them to the other, I began to feel
slightly uncomfortable. Reluctantly, I gave them the first two
lines:

"I'm fourteen now. They call me Sam.

But nobody really knows who I am . . ."

It was enough, I decided. I didn't want to recite the entire
poem, even if I did know it all by heart—and by soul.

None of us said anything for a second.

"Could I read it sometime?" Mr. Daniels inquired gently.

"I'll see if I can get you a copy of the last issue," I offered.

"That would be great," Mr. Daniels replied.

I dropped my eyes and moved the birthstone ring on my left
hand back and forth against the knuckle.

They must have gotten the hint. They stopped asking about
the poem.

"Melody, what else do you like to do for fun?" Mr. Daniels
asked. "Movies? Shopping?"

I shook my head. "Horses," I replied. "I take riding lessons in
the summer, and I volunteer at the stables."

"You volunteer?"

"Yes. There's a program there—for kids," I said. "Kids who are handicapped."

Miss Weatherall stopped taking notes. "The riding-therapy program?"

I nodded.

"It's wonderful!" she exclaimed. "I had a niece with cerebral palsy who rode a horse in that program. I think she still does. Her name is Carly."

I smiled big-time because I knew who Carly was and because the program *was* wonderful. It was amazing what the horses did for some of those kids.

"What do you do there?" Mr. Daniels asked.

"Everything," I said, turning my hands up. "Feed the horses, turn them out in the pasture, do barn cleanup. When it's time for the horses to come in, I help get them. I groom, tack up for the riders, lead them around the ring. Sometimes I'm a side-walker—those are the people who make sure the kids stay on. You know, because some of them have muscles that aren't developed, and it's hard for them to control themselves. I help to make sure they don't fall off or anything."

"I see," he said.

He started asking about Mom then. Where she worked and when she got home.

"She gets home from the nursery about dinnertime," I replied.

The questions got odd after that.

"Are you at home by yourself much?" Mr. Daniels asked.

"Hardly at all. I'm either at school or at the stables. I can walk there from my house."

"Do you *try* not to be at home alone?"

I frowned because why would he want to know that?

When I didn't answer, he asked, "What are the rules at home? What is expected of you?"

I shrugged. "To do my homework and keep my room clean, I guess. I wash the dishes when Mom asks me to, and my brother, Cade, takes out the garbage and mows the lawn."

"How does your father react when you break the rules? Or when Cade doesn't do what he's told to do?"

What? Where was he going with *those* questions? I frowned and didn't answer.

"Does your father have a temper? Does he ever hurt Cade or you?"

"No!" I exclaimed.

"Are you ever afraid of your father, Melody?"

My mouth went dry. I stared at Mr. Daniels.

"Melody, do you have pets? Do they ever get in trouble? Has anyone ever been mean to them?"

I felt myself standing up, gathering my books. I didn't want to answer any more of their questions.

But they continued: "What happens when your parents don't agree? Do they argue?"

"I have to go now," I said. I could hear my voice waver.

I hoped they wouldn't stop me as I moved toward the door.

But Mr. Daniels stood and reached for me. When he did, his jacket fell open, and I could see the gun he had tucked in a black leather holster.

"Melody," he said, grabbing my arm, "are you afraid to go home?"

⑤ Claire

Dear Mrs. Fernandez:

You asked me to tell you what Mr. Mattero did and all the details so I will try. Thank you because I would be so embarrassed to be saying all this out loud. <u>Please</u> don't call my parents until I tell you to because they don't know anything about it. We have been like scared to death to say a single word to anyone.

It all began at lunch Monday. Monday is when Mr. Mattero came to our table in the cafeteria and asked did anyone in study hall want to put away Peter Pan stuff. I wasn't in the play because of the flu. I missed six days of school because of the flu, and my mother thought I shouldn't overdo it. But my best friend Jenna Cartwright was a pirate and my other best friend Suzanne Elmore, her and her mother helped make costumes.

So we were eating lunch. Actually Jenna and
Suzanne were eating lunch. I already ate my apple
and was sucking on a Tic Tac because I am on a
diet and have lost eighteen pounds since sixth
grade. Jenna said we should volunteer to help Mr.
Mattero so we raised our hands and he said great
did we need a note but we didn't think so.

Last period we signed out of study hall and went
to the music room, where Mrs. Reicher and another
mom showed us what to do. Mrs. Reicher said to
fold up the Indian costumes and tuck the wigs with
braids into a Ziploc bag and put them all in one
plastic box. Then she said to take the lost boy costumes off the hangers and fold each one neat and
put them in another tub.

We started working. Mrs. Reicher and the other
mom who I think might be Carlisa's mother stood on
the side of the room under the wall clock and Mrs.
Reicher started bragging about her daughter Marcie
who was Wendy in the play. She went on and on
about what a fantastic voice Marcie had, blah,
blah, blah, and how Marcie was having voice lessons
from a music professor at the university and how she
might go to a special arts high school in Baltimore.

After those mothers left, Jenna said let's try on
the Indian dresses for fun. Suzanne and I said do it

over our jeans, but Jenna said it wouldn't look right
so we got undressed behind the piano in case someone came in the door.

 We were halfway undressed when Mr. Mattero
came back. We only had our underwear on so we
held the dresses in front of us. We were really
scared. Mr. Mattero started laughing. He came over
and gave Jenna a hug. Then he put his arms around
me too and patted me on the butt. He tried to hug
Suzanne. He ran his hand up and down her back
and touched the back of her bra. She said, "Please
don't do that, Mr. Mattero" and started crying.

 When he walked away, he was still laughing. We
were scared. We said let's get out of there. We got
dressed and went back to study hall. That is what
happened.

 Claire Montague

6 Melody

MR. DANIELS SAW ME STARING AT HIS GUN.

"It's all right," he assured me, releasing my arm. "I'm a police detective."

I took a step backward. "But I don't understand. Why are you asking me these questions? What kind of a survey is this?"

"Look, Melody," Detective Daniels reached toward me again, but I took another step backward. "Like I told you, we travel from school to school making sure students are safe."

"It's true, Melody," Miss Weatherall chimed in. "That's all we're doing."

But I wasn't sure I believed either one of them anymore. "I'm safe," I declared. "May I go now?"

Mr. Daniels dropped his hand. "Of course," he said, but he sounded frustrated. "You can go, Melody."

Suddenly, Miss Weatherall was on her feet, too, reaching into her pocketbook and offering me a small white card. "Do not hesitate to call if you want to talk."

"Wait a minute." Mr. Daniels—*Detective* Daniels—snatched the card before it was in my hand. "I don't have my cards with me." He pulled a ballpoint pen from his pocket and wrote on the back of it. "That's my cell phone number. You can call me, too. Anytime."

I accepted the card, then I hustled myself out of there. Last period was almost over, and already the office secretary was coming on the intercom with end–of–school announcements. *"The girls' lacrosse team should go directly to their bus for the away game. Boys' lacrosse report to the field for practice."*

A few kids were moving into the hallways, but most were still in class awaiting the final bell. I was glad I had a head start.

Some days, if I stayed late for play practice or the magazine, I rode home from school with my father. But Wednesdays, when I volunteered at the stable, I always took the bus. So I headed to my locker for my jacket and to grab the homework books I needed.

Cindy Jarmon and I arrived at our side–by–side lockers at the same time. When we were little, Cindy was in my Brownie troop. I used to go to her birthday parties. But she is Miss Popularity now, a cheerleader, too. I try not to hold that against her, and usually we get along fine. We even say hi to each other in the mornings. Then we get our stuff and go our separate ways. But that day, while I stood spinning the dial to my combination, she asked me what had happened.

"What do you mean?"

She screwed up her face. "Like, what happened to your dad?"

I was still confused by the session I'd just had with Detective Daniels and Miss Weatherall, and it annoyed me that Cindy was being so nosy. Quickly, I pushed the small white card I'd just been given into my jeans pocket. Even if my dad *was* in some kind of trouble, Cindy didn't care; she just wanted to gossip.

"Nothing happened," I said. As far as I knew, that was true.

The announcements continued: *"There will be no jazz band practice or instrument lessons after school today."*

Why no jazz band? I wondered. Dad would never cancel jazz band a week before the competition!

"All students who are in the band, or are scheduled for a lesson with Mr. Mattero, please report to the library."

Startled, my lips parted in surprise. I looked at Cindy who was staring at me. But I pulled myself together fast, reached into my locker for my jacket, slammed the metal door shut, then spun around and raced for the bus.

I took a seat near the back and was grateful when no one else sat beside me. Our bus wasn't crowded, thank goodness. After we turned out of the school driveway and headed down the highway, I reached into my pants pocket for the little white card I'd just been given. Glancing around, I saw that no one was looking, so I took my time reading it.

Janice Weatherall

Child Welfare Investigations

Patuxent County Department of Social Services

Her phone and Fax numbers were listed. On the flip side was Detective Daniels inked–in cell phone number.

Frowning, I stared at the card. Why would these people want to talk to *me*? Were they worried about something happening at my school? Were they worried about someone in particular? Was this somehow connected to Dad? It was such a bizarre day. See? I still hadn't figured it out.

At the end of Bellevue Avenue, I got off the bus with three other kids who live in my neighborhood and walked up the sidewalk toward home. It was a warm spring day. Almost every yard I passed had some bright yellow daffodils blooming. One of my neighbors was even out mowing his lawn, a welcome sound, even if it was kind of early. But I wasn't in a mood to enjoy a beautiful afternoon.

When I crested the hill on Bellevue Avenue, I could see ahead to our house and how Dad's old red Mercury Cougar was parked in our driveway beside my mother's ancient orange Volvo station wagon. Things were getting more and more strange. Why was he home? Mom, too. She worked Wednesdays at the nursery. I quickened my pace.

When I opened the side door to our kitchen, my dad's loud,

angry voice carried clearly from the back of the house. "I don't know! I have absolutely no idea!"

Mom's purse and car keys were on the counter. I set down my backpack and walked softly to the doorway of the family room, where I could see both of my parents outside on the back deck. The sliding doors that opened onto the deck were cracked open. Mom sat in one of four chairs at the umbrella table while Dad paced back and forth, his shirttails hanging out, his tie askew. He was running a hand across his head fitfully, the way he does at band rehearsal when he's frustrated because we're not playing together. His other hand held something against his face.

"Fred, take it easy," Mom said, motioning for Dad to slow down. "Go over it one more time. What, exactly, did Helena say to you?"

Helena is the first name of Mrs. Fernandez, our principal, but Dad has known her for years. Mr. and Mrs. Fernandez have even come to our house for dinner.

Dad stopped pacing and sat down in a chair in front of my mother. I could see that it was an ice pack he pressed against his jaw. Neither one of my parents knew I was home. Quietly, I took another couple steps forward.

"Beginning of third period, Helena called me down to the office," Dad started explaining.

"Why didn't she wait until those girls were out of school?" my mother interrupted. "You wouldn't have gotten slugged if she'd gotten them out of there first!"

Pausing, Dad looked at her. "You asked me what happened, Mary."

"I'm sorry, Fred," Mom apologized in a soft voice. "Go on. Tell me. Helena called you to the office."

Dad took a deep breath and let it out. "Right. So she called me down. She said we needed to talk. I was in the music room with Mellie, and I was thinking to myself, 'Oh, boy, what did I do this time?' And the only thing I could think of is that I gave that kid, Brett Johnson, a detention for not showing up at band practice last week. He was really ticked off about it, you know? But it's less than two weeks before the competition in Virginia, and he knew I needed everybody there.

"When I got to the office I asked Helena, 'Is it that kid, Brett Johnson?' She said, 'It's worse than that. Have a seat, Fred.' So I sat down. She was having a hard time getting it out. Finally, she said that three girls, three seventh-grade girls, had come to the office and complained that I had touched them inappropriately in the band rehearsal room on Monday."

"Monday. Two days ago?" Mom asked.

"Yeah."

"In the band rehearsal room?" Mom repeated.

"That's right. She said she separated them right away and had them write down everything. She said their stories matched, that they were identical."

Dad sighed, and there was a moment when neither of my parents said anything. They were turned away from me, and I couldn't tell if they were even looking at each other or not. Harmony, our black and white cat, rubbed up against my legs, but I didn't reach down to pet her because I was straining to hear.

Calmly, my mother asked, "Fred, what did the girls say you did?"

Dad started shaking his head.

"Fred, what did they say?" Mom pressed.

"They said they were undressed in the rehearsal room, trying on some *Peter Pan* outfits, and that I walked in on them, hugged them, rubbed one of them on the back, and touched another on the . . . on her behind."

There were a few more seconds of silence. Then my mother asked in a soft voice. "Did you do it, Fred?"

Just then, Harmony jumped up on the counter beside me and knocked over a plastic tumbler. I grabbed for it, but it clattered to the floor.

"Mellie! You're home!" Mom exclaimed as both my parents rushed to the doorway.

"Yes," I said, standing up and placing the tumbler back on the counter. I scooped up Harmony and held her close.

Dad wasn't holding the ice pack against his face anymore, and I could see how the area around one eye was kind of red and puffed up.

Mom looked from me to Dad and back to me. "Were you listening?"

I nodded. "Dad said some seventh–graders accused him of something."

Mom's eyes slid sideways, to look sadly at my father. "And an angry parent hit him in the face."

Dad held up the hand that wasn't holding the ice pack. "Look, Mellie," he said. "I didn't touch those girls. I have no idea what's behind this!"

"Then we have nothing to be afraid of," my mother said calmly. "Everything will be all right."

But everything was not going to be all right. Not by a long shot. The next thing we knew someone was ringing the doorbell, and it turned out to be Mrs. Fernandez.

Mom invited her in and asked her to come sit in the living room, but my principal came only as far as the umbrella stand in the front hall. "I'd better not," she said, handing Dad an envelope.

My father took the envelope, but didn't open it right away.

"Fred, listen," Mrs. Fernandez said, stuffing her hands into the pockets of her trench coat. "I don't know what has happened, or what is going to happen, but you know as well as I do, the school system has a policy. They have rules. And I need to follow the rules."

"But I didn't do anything, Helena!" Dad exclaimed, suddenly coming to life. "I can't deny I was in the rehearsal room with those girls—I *was!* I asked them to put the costumes away. But nothing happened in there. Nothing!"

"Fred, please understand. I am not casting judgment. I am following procedures."

The way she said that, we knew we couldn't ask her for more.

Mrs. Fernandez pulled her hands out of her pockets, held one up to say good-bye, and left.

As soon as the door closed, we turned to Dad. He ripped open the envelope, unfolded the letter inside, and we crowded around him to read it silently, together:

Dear Mr. Frederick Mattero,

This letter is to notify you that you are being placed on administrative leave with pay. In the meantime you are not permitted on Oakdale Middle School grounds, and you are ordered to have no contact with any of the teachers or students there.

Sincerely,

Helena Fernandez, Principal

7 Claire

SUZANNE'S MOTHER WAS HYSTERICAL.

"What did he do to my baby? My poor baby! I can't believe this!" she cried. She had folded her arms around Suzanne—she practically smothered her—and she was making one heck of a giant racket, if you ask me. I was embarrassed for Suzanne, I really was. What a spectacle. And *her*—Suzanne—not saying a word, just standing there like she went mute or something.

This was before Jenna's dad stormed in and took a swing at Mr. Mattero. But it's not like Mr. Mattero was looking for a fight. All he did was walk by the guidance office, where we were standing with our parents, and someone whispered, "That's him—that's Fred Mattero!" Jenna's dad bolted out of the door like lightning and took after him down the hall.

We spilled out the door to watch. Even Suzanne freed herself from her mother so she could see. It wasn't a very pretty sight. Kind of scary, actually, the way Jenna's dad grabbed Mr. Mattero from behind and hit him in the face with his fist. Mr. Mattero fell against the lockers and groaned. He put his hands up on his jaw while Jenna's dad stood there, hollering at him, "You pervert!" It looked like he was getting ready to punch him again, too, only two teachers, Mr. Saunders and Mr. Fellows, came running up behind Jenna's dad and grabbed his arms just in time.

Seemed like all hell was breaking loose, and boy, we hadn't planned on that. Not Jenna, not Suzanne, and not me—none of us even thought our parents were going to get called in to school, never mind overreact the way they did. We just thought Mrs. Fernandez would move us out of that music class. That we'd go to study hall instead and that eventually there would be some sort of a parent-kid conference and that would be it.

"Come on, Claire, we're going home," Mom said, taking my hand and pulling me toward the door.

"Please! Don't go yet!" Mrs. Fernandez protested, opening her arms like she was trying to herd us into a corner. "I need you both to stay—"

"No," Mom told her in no uncertain terms. She whirled around. "I'm taking Claire home." And we left. We didn't even stop at my locker or anything, we just hightailed it on out of there.

Mom put her arm around my shoulders as we walked out of school. I could see our van parked in a visitor's slot. Even though our parents went off the deep end, I have to say it felt nice having Mom rush in and whisk me away like that. But I also felt a little bad that Jenna's dad actually hit Mr. Mattero, and a little guilty, too, on account of I know it's not easy for my mom to just drop everything at home. Because of my little brother mainly.

"Where's Corky?" I asked her as we climbed into the two front seats. I knew my sister, Isabelle, was in nursery school, but I wondered what she'd done with my little brother on such short notice. He didn't have such a good morning and had stayed home from kindergarten.

"He's next door," she said as we buckled ourselves in.

"You left him with Mrs. Butters?" I asked, unable to believe it. I mean, Mrs. Butters is about ninety years old and deaf as a doorknob.

Mom did not look at me as she started up the van. "Claire, they called and said it was an emergency. What choice did I have?"

And suddenly I had a flash of something else in her voice. Like maybe she didn't think it *was* an emergency. Like maybe she was ticked off about having to come to school. So maybe she didn't rush us out of school for my sake—but to get home quick and get Corky back in the house where he was safe. But why would that surprise me? Everything my family did revolved around Corky. What we needed to do for Corky.

Angrily, I crossed my arms.

"I'm sorry, Claire." Mom reached over and touched my arm as she slowed our car at the blinking light in front of school. It's like she can read my mind sometimes. "What happened to you and Jenna and Suzanne is terrible. It's awful. I mean, I hope they fire that man."

"Fire him?" I was, like, astonished that my mother would even suggest such a thing. "Fire Mr. Mattero?"

"Of course." My mother put both hands on the steering wheel, focused ahead, and took off down the road. "A man like that should *not* be in the position of teaching children—or even of being around them."

My mouth dropped open as we cruised down the highway. I turned to stare out the window at all the stuff I see every day from the bus, but it blurred by: the animal hospital in the little blue house, the tattoo parlor with the dragon on the window, the sleazy pawnshop next door to the pizza place.

"They don't need to fire him," I said quietly, pulling the sleeves of my sweatshirt over my hands. "We just wanted to, like, be moved out of his class so we don't have to deal with him anymore." I swung my head around to look at Mom because I didn't want her to misunderstand. "You know, because of what Mr. Mattero did."

"But, Claire, look—a person like that cannot be allowed around children because what if he does it again? And what if he doesn't stop with the kind of touching that he did to you girls?"

Suddenly this terrible expression absolutely took over my mother's face. Her brow got all wrinkled, and her lips pressed together, like she was on the verge of crying, the way she looks when Corky does something he hasn't done before, like hitting his head on the floor over and over. Only this time Mom's worry—for once—was for me.

"No, it wasn't very nice," I agreed with her, fueling the concern. "He really scared me, Mom."

"Claire, I'm so sorry this happened to you." She glanced at me, and I could see tears in her eyes. "It really makes me angry."

"Yeah. Me, too," I agreed. I mean, I was really egging her on.

"They'd better take some action on this," Mom insisted. "The school. Mrs. Fernandez. The police. They'd better do a good investigation."

"The police?" I almost laughed because I thought she was joking.

When Mom stopped at the next traffic light, she turned so we could look at each other. She stuck a finger under her sunglasses, to wipe at her eye. "Claire, we may have to file charges because what Mr. Mattero did was against the law."

Whoa. I didn't know that either! I had no idea it was *that* serious. You know, touching someone that way? Sure, sure. I knew it was wrong. In fifth grade a policeman came and talked to our class about the good-touch/bad-touch stuff. And how no one had a right to touch your privates. But this wasn't the same thing—was it? And anyway, I sure didn't remember that it could like get you arrested or anything like that.

I blinked, but I didn't know what to say so I didn't say anything. I just shut my mouth, pulled back, and stared into my lap. Stunned, I guess. A little stunned, as I bit my thumbnail again, not even caring if I made my finger bleed.

When the light turned green, Mom drove a ways and then turned off the highway into one of the million shopping centers that are in my town. She parked at the Dairy Mart. "Do you want to run in and get a hot dog for lunch?"

Wide-eyed, I looked at her. I loved hot dogs, but I hadn't had one in months, not since I went on my diet. Mom didn't even buy hot dogs anymore. But not on account of my diet. It was because of Corky, who can't eat, like, dairy or wheat or even eggs anymore, and you never really know what's in a hot dog, my mom says.

"It's all right." I started to shake my head because hot dogs had too many calories—like over a hundred for just one, never mind the bun.

"Here—" Mom shoved a five-dollar bill into my hand. "Run in and get yourself a hot dog and a Diet Coke and whatever you want with what's left. Some gum or something."

I took the five, but I hesitated. I knew this was sympathy money. Feel-sorry-for-Claire money.

Mom reached over and closed my hand around the money. "Go ahead, honey."

I figured I deserved something for what I'd just been through, so I undid my seat belt and opened the car door. Inside the store, just like the old days, I bought myself a hot dog, pumped on some mustard, ketchup, and relish from the

containers, grabbed a cold can of Diet Coke from the fridge
case, and picked out two packs of sugarless gum. Even at that,
there was some change, which I put in my sweatshirt pocket
because my jeans were so dang tight I could hardly put anything in those pockets.

I knew Mom expected me to eat in the van, before we got
home and Corky got a whiff of it. So as soon as I got my seat
belt back on, I unwrapped the hot dog, pushed it up between
the pieces of bun so I'd only bite the meat part and not the
bread, and started eating. When I was done, I wrapped up the
uneaten roll really tight in the leftover wax paper so Mom
couldn't see and stuffed the wad deep in the trash can when we
entered the house.

At home, while Mom rushed off to pick up both of the kids,
I took my soda and went up into my room to change out of
my jeans. I put on some loose, comfy sweatpants and flopped
on my bed wondering if Suzanne's mother was still blubbering
away in the school office and what was happening with Jenna.
What was *she* thinking? Did she know her father would show
up at school? Did he apologize to Mr. Mattero for hitting him?
I shuddered when I thought of that and rolled over to hug my
stuffed platypus.

It took Mom a long time to come home. The house was
stone quiet without her and the kids. I heard the mantel clock
downstairs gong twice for two o'clock. I heard a squirrel scurry

across the roof. I heard the heating coils under the baseboard click. I didn't like being alone. It made me think too much.

So I got up to put some music on my CD player and to call Jenna from the phone in my room, but no answer, so I left a message for her to call me back. I set the phone on my bed in case it rang and reached over to pick up a magazine I had dropped on the floor the night before. I was just, like, scanning the stuff on the cover: "The Sexiest New Jeans." "Shoes, Shoes, and More Shoes." "The Surprising New Way to Find Your Perfect Guy." "Could a Cult Be Targeting You?" Then I started flipping through the pages and was checking out those new chrome-colored nail polishes when Mom came home and called upstairs.

A man and woman I didn't know were standing with Mom, Corky, and Izzy in the front hall. Corky made a beeline for me and grabbed me around the knees. "Hey, buddy," I said. He squeezed really hard.

"This is Mr. Daniels from the police department," Mom said. "And this is Miss Weatherall with the child welfare department. They need to talk to you, Claire, about what happened at school."

It didn't look as though I had a choice, so I pried Corky's hands from my legs and went into the living room, where we sat down. "Where's Care going?" Izzy kept asking (that's what she calls me—Care). "She's going to talk with the people," Mom told her while she brought us glasses of water. "Who those peoples? Where's Care?" Izzy kept asking while Mom dragged her and Corky off to the backyard.

When they were gone, I told Mr. Daniels the same exact things I wrote down for Mrs. Fernandez. Then they asked me a bunch of questions about Jenna and Suzanne, like about how long we had been friends and stuff.

"Don't be afraid or worry about going back to school," Mr. Daniels said when he was done. "Mr. Mattero won't be allowed back until there has been a thorough investigation."

"He won't?" I asked.

"No. You're perfectly safe going back to school," Miss Weatherall said. She wore clothes like my grandmother would wear, only she didn't look that old. When she closed up her little notebook, I swallowed hard. Because I was also thinking, If Mr. Mattero couldn't come back to school, who would teach music?

"Thanks for your time, Claire," Mr. Daniels said.

Miss Weatherall handed me a little white card. She said it had her phone number on it, just in case I needed to talk to her.

"*My* number is on the back, Claire," Mr. Daniels said. "You can call either one of us. You know, if you forgot to tell us something—anything. Please feel free to call. Anytime."

After they left, Mom came rushing back in saying she had forgotten some appointment she had for one of the kids and had to rush off. "Can you make us up a batch of chicken tenders for supper?" Mom asked. "Please, Claire, could you do that while I'm gone? Daddy's late tonight. We'll save him some dinner."

My dad was almost always late on account of his commute into Washington, D.C. Every day he got bogged down in traffic. Sometimes it took him hours to get home, and we don't live, like, that far away.

"Sure," I told Mom. "I'll make some tenders."

Corky was pulling on my hands because he wanted me to go, too.

Mom warned, "I don't want anyone over while I'm gone. Not Suzanne—and especially not Jenna. No one."

"Why not?" I asked her, pulling my hand free from Corky.

Izzy ran out the door while Mom threw her purse over her shoulder and grabbed my little brother, swinging him up into her arms. He whined and struggled to get down because he hates going places. "I just want to let things calm down a little," Mom said.

"Okay," I told her, but in a weak voice and secretly rolling my eyes because it irritated me, my mom's attitude. She is always looking for an excuse why I can't be with Jenna.

Mom looked like she was getting ready to say something else, so I said, "'Bye, Mom. 'Bye, Cork. 'Bye Iz," and closed the door.

First thing I did, I picked up the remote in the family room and cruised the channels until I found an old episode of *Hercules*. Then I put the remote on the counter and went to work in the kitchen, where I could still see the TV.

After I'd cut up all that disgusting raw chicken and cleaned off the cutting board with soap and water, I realized my mother didn't have any flour left for me to roll the pieces in. I moaned out loud because that meant I had to like make it from scratch, the special flour Corky needs, and let me tell you, it is a pain in the butt because you have to mix up like ten different things: rice flour, soy flour, garbanzo-bean flour, tapioca starch, a whole bunch of stuff. There's a recipe on our flour jar.

I got it done though. I made the chicken tenders and put them in a bowl with a snap lid and stuck them in the fridge. Corky loves his chicken tenders. On chicken days he eats them with spinach and yams. I washed my hands to get that chicken and flour stuff off. Then I wiped off the counter. I knew I had saved my mother about half an hour of work.

Still, I was feeling a little bit down over all the stuff that had happened at school and the talk with Mr. Daniels and the fact that police were involved and that Jenna still hadn't called back. So, to cheer myself up, I turned off the TV—*Hercules* was over—and went back to my room to put some eyeliner on and French-braid my hair.

8 Melody

POOR DAD. He slumped into the big easy chair in our living room, leaned his head back, and, with one hand holding the ice pack against his jaw, used his other hand to cover his eyes. He seemed so defeated, so completely blown away by what had happened.

My mother refolded the letter from Mrs. Fernandez, tucked it back in its envelope, and placed it on top of the microwave. If only we could have put the whole situation away as easily.

"What are we going to do now?" I asked quietly.

She shook her head. "I don't know. I don't know what we do next." She glanced at the clock on the stove. "But you need to get on with things, Mellie. They're expecting you at the barn, aren't they?"

"I'm supposed to help tack up at three-thirty."

"You'd better go then." She touched my arm. "Go ahead."

Upstairs in my room, I dropped my backpack on my bed and changed into barn clothes—jeans, a T-shirt, thick socks, and leather paddock boots. Harmony followed me upstairs and jumped on my bed, kneading the comforter until I went over and scratched her under the chin. When I came down the stairs, I saw Mom and Dad sitting together in the living room, but I didn't disturb them. I went out through the kitchen, closed the door softly, and left.

The pasture for the Trefoil Stables, where I volunteer, is right behind our neighborhood. In fact, the land we live on was once part of Trefoil Farm, but now all that's left of the old farm is twenty acres and the barn. It's like a little oasis of green surrounded by housing developments like ours, all of them pretty much the same. Rolling hills of identical rooflines. It's that way all over Wallinsburg.

On my volunteer days, all I have to do is walk to the back end of our lot, squeeze between the bars of the fence, and walk across the field. When I got to the barn, horses for the afternoon classes were already waiting, some of them tied to a rail outside the stable, others standing inside at cross ties in the walkway between their stalls.

I saw Nova, the pretty bay that I rode for lessons in the summer, and stopped to give her a pat on the neck. She moved her head up and down—I hope it was because she recognized me, but probably not. There are a lot of people at the barns, a lot of volunteers like me. We all get riding lessons at reduced rates, which is the only way my parents could afford to let me ride.

Mrs. Dandridge, the volunteer coordinator, spotted me and waved.

I waved back but I didn't call out hi or anything. I was still mixed up inside and didn't know what I wanted to be on the outside. At the barn at least, no one would know about what had happened at my school.

"Hey there, Melody," Mrs. Dandridge said. "I'm going to have you groom and tack up Misty today. That little boy—Alexander—is coming for a four o'clock class."

I smiled a little at the mention of this little boy, then crossed my fingers and held them up. "Let's hope it works today," I said. During his first two lessons Alexander had refused to get anywhere near Misty, let alone ride him. He wouldn't even come into the barn to *see* the horses. He was a cute little boy though, about four, maybe five years old, with dark hair and big brown eyes. Because he was so afraid, Mrs. Dandridge asked me to take him inside the office, where we spent his first two lessons watching videos about horses.

Volunteers like me don't know too much about the kids we work with. Usually just their first names and a little bit about what's wrong with them. For example, they may have cerebral palsy, or Down syndrome. They may have suffered a traumatic brain injury, like one little girl we had who was hit by a car. Or they might be visually or hearing impaired. Some of the kids are mentally retarded, some have muscular dystrophy, and some come to riding therapy because of strokes, which really surprised me. I didn't realize young children could have strokes.

I wasn't sure what Alexander's disability was. Physically, he seemed fine. But he didn't say much. The only thing I did know was that he loved Superman so much that the first day he came he wore a dingy old baby blanket, fastened with a big safety pin, around his shoulders. His mother said it was his "flying cape."

Misty, a small light gray gelding with black stockings, stood patiently waiting at one of the cross ties in the barn. I made my way into the tack room, grabbed the horse's box full of grooming brushes, and walked over to say hello. I rubbed Misty's nose and patted his neck. He was one of the gentlest horses in the entire barn. "You ready for your lesson today?"

Misty hadn't been ridden earlier, so I took the currycomb and vigorously made circular motions all over him, avoiding his face and legs, to loosen the dust and dead hair. Next, I used the curry mitt to do his face and legs. Then I pulled with a firmer brush and long, hard strokes to get the loose dirt and hair off. And I wondered as I did this: Why in the world would some seventh-graders make up a nasty story about my father? Did he do something to make them angry?

Finally, I used a softer brush to finish off Misty's face and legs, all the time thinking that my father must be going nuts, realizing that he would be losing valuable rehearsal time before the annual band competition. Every year he took the band down to Virginia to compete, and for the past five years they had returned with the first-place trophy.

When the brushing was done, I returned to the tack room, ran a clean washrag under warm water in the sink, and used the cloth to wipe around Misty's eyes and the rest of his face. Stupid seventh-graders, I started thinking. They probably made it all up—for fun! Man, if I found out who those jerks were, I would tell them a thing or two! I stopped wiping and stared at the wooden barn floor wondering just how mad I could get and what I might actually do. Grab them? Yell? Spit at them?

The last part of grooming was to clean the hooves. I reached for the hoof pick, then turned with my back to Misty's front and picked up one of his front legs the way a blacksmith does so I could clean out the area inside his shoes. It was when I set his front leg down that I saw little Alexander and his mom approaching the barn door. I couldn't believe he'd already come this close to the horses. It was a good sign.

"Hey there!" I waved to him.

Alexander didn't speak, but his mother smiled back.

"Are you going to ride today?" I called over to him.

The boy buried his face against his mother.

Maybe not, I thought to myself, biting my lip and hoping I hadn't come on too cheerful. While I finished the hooves, I noticed how Alexander was sneaking glances at me. And suddenly, I had an idea.

When I took the grooming tools back to the tack room, I stopped Mrs. Dandridge. "I just saw Alexander," I told her. "He seems really afraid, so I wondered—what about the finger paints?"

"Great idea!" Her face lit up with approval.

We found the paints on a shelf near the saddles, and while Mrs. Dandridge fetched water and a towel, I walked to where Alexander was watching from outside the barn door. His mother shrugged and flashed me a hopeless look.

I smiled back. "We had an idea," I said, kneeling down so I was at Alexander's level. When he turned his face away, I tugged gently on his sleeve. "Do you like to finger paint?"

Alexander kept his head turned.

"He *loves* to paint," his mother confirmed.

"Misty wondered if you would like to paint *him*!" I told the little boy.

Slowly, Alexander turned his head to look at me.

"I'm not kidding. Misty *loves* to be painted."

Alexander peeked up at his mother, and she gave him an encouraging smile and a nod.

I gave him the paints and told him to come with me. This meant he would have to actually step foot in the barn, which he hadn't done yet. But it worked; Alexander followed me to where Misty stood.

When Mrs. Dandridge appeared with a bowl of water and a towel, we moved quickly so as not to lose momentum. I opened three jars and dipped two of my fingers in red. "Watch," I said, smearing the red paint on the side of Misty's big gray, furry belly.

Alexander grinned. His wide eyes sparkled. He came over and put three fingers in the jar of blue, then walked right up to the horse and made a broad blue stripe over my red blob.

"That's great!" I cheered. "More color!"

Alexander dipped his fingers in the jar of yellow and made another stripe parallel to the blue one. Then he took both hands and rubbed the paint around and around, all over Misty's side. The horse nickered softly. His big belly shook. Alexander jumped back.

"See? He said he likes it! The paint feels good!" I told him. "It's like getting a massage!"

Alexander chuckled and continued painting, making huge spirals of color all over the horse's side. A few other people in the barn came over to watch, and pretty soon Alexander and Misty had a small audience. For twenty minutes he painted the horse. When it was over, after he had washed his hands and cleaned up, he came back to stroke Misty on the nose and see his artwork once more before leaving with his mother.

"A definite step forward," Mrs. Dandridge said, putting an arm around my shoulder and squeezing it. "That was the perfect idea, Melody! Now he's not afraid. Next week, maybe, he'll help you brush the horse!"

"Thanks," I said. I was pretty pleased myself with how it had

turned out. I unhooked Misty from the cross ties and started to
lead him out back where I would hose him off, when all of a
sudden, Alexander came running back into the barn, full speed.
"Hey, slow down," I said, not wanting him to scare the horses.
But Alexander kept running, and, when he got to me, he threw
his arms around my legs. A big hug, then a sprint back to his
mother.

I led the horse back out of the barn, and I couldn't help but
wonder if my father hadn't hugged someone at school in the
same spontaneous way. Or patted someone on the back? Or,
like Mrs. Dandridge had just done to me, squeezed someone's
shoulders because they had done a good job? Had my father,
in perfect innocence, touched someone who turned that touch
against him?

Why? Why would someone do that to my dad?

I stood, holding Misty's lead rope as something else
occurred to me: Would the kids at school know about what
had happened? Would they think my father actually *did* something to those girls?

What was going to happen to my dad?

And what was going to happen to me—to my family?

"Dee!" I turned around and through a warm wall of tears saw
Alexander waving as he called out the last part of my name.

9 Claire

WHOEVER WOULD HAVE THOUGHT two bombs could hit in the same day?

What I found out about Jenna that night absolutely blew me away. It made me think I ought to be writing a script for a movie or something . . .

Okay. Okay. Back up for a second. So I had just finished my hair, my two French braids, except that I have these stupid layers, remember, and all these wispy ends that I can't get into the braids so they end up hanging down the sides of my face, but actually that's sort of cool, so, really, I don't mind. Anyway, braids were done. I had finished my Diet Coke, which was all I could have for dinner on account of the hot dog. And I was lying on my bed waiting for Mom and the kids to come home when Jenna called.

"Claire—"

"Hey. Hi."

"So did those police people show up at your house?"

"Mr. Daniels and that woman?"

"Yeah. They were here, too," Jenna said.

"It was kind of creepy, wasn't it?"

"No. It wasn't creepy," Jenna disagreed. "I mean, I just repeated what I wrote down at school. Didn't you?"

"Duh. Of course, I did. I mean, what did you think I did?"

Pause.

"Look, can you come over, Claire? My dad's bringing a pizza."

"I don't think so," I told her. I didn't want to eat pizza. Well, I did, but I couldn't. You know, on account of my diet. "I already ate," I told her. But typical Jenna, she would not take no for an answer.

"Claire, you have to come over. I've got your backpack. You left it at school!"

"But that was going to be my excuse for not doing my homework!"

Jenna wasn't laughing. Her voice got small. "Claire, please come. My dad is really upset about what happened."

"Yeah. My mom's pretty angry, too. And can you believe Suzanne's mother at school?"

"Wasn't that awful? Her mother is, like, so fragile," Jenna said. "I just talked to Suzanne. You won't believe what her mother's going to do next."

"What?"

"I won't tell you unless you come over."

"I'll call Suzanne myself."

"You can't! Her mother won't let her back on the phone!"

"Jenna!"

"Claire!"

"Please come and I'll tell you everything," Jenna promised.

Big long sigh. "All right." I gave in. See? Jenna always got her way. "I'll leave my mom a note."

Jenna lived about two blocks away. There is a sidewalk connecting our neighborhoods, mine with houses that are all the same except for which side the garage is on, and hers with town houses that all have cute little balconies but no garages. Exactly halfway there is a little bridge that crosses a drainage ditch between the houses and the town houses. Sometimes we meet there. But Jenna wasn't there to meet me that day.

When I got to her family's town house, her father was driving up with the pizza they were having for dinner. He revved up the motor of his red sports car once before turning it off.

"Hi there, Claire," he greeted me through the open window.

"Hey," I said back.

Mostly, Jenna's dad is a pretty nice guy. Fit—very fit because he works out at the gym every day. I don't think I've ever seen him when he wasn't wearing tight jeans with a snug white T-shirt tucked in. I think it's his uniform, what he wears to work at a construction company or something. There's always a hard hat in the back window of his little red car.

"Awful what happened to you girls at school," he said, slamming the door to his car with his foot because he had the pizza box in one hand and a big bottle of Coke in the other.

I waited for him.

"Guess you heard I busted that guy in the face for what he done," he said.

"Yeah, I was there," I told him. But I didn't say it with a big smile or anything.

He grunted as he walked past me, like he was still angry. "Next time I'll kill the son of a bitch," he snarled. Turning, he pointed the bottle of Coke at me. "I'm not kidding, Claire. He touches one of you girls again, he's dead."

See, this is the thing that scares me about Jenna's dad. He has this incredible temper. You hear on the news about these wacko people doing crazy things, and I worry Jenna's dad could be one of them. He's a little bit scary, and I didn't want to see Mr. Mattero get killed over this. I'm serious! So already, walking in, I was starting to get nervous.

Jenna ran right up to me and gave me a hug. A big hug. "Thanks for coming, Cwaire." She talked a little funny, and with a lisp, because she had her Crest Strips on. But she looked really nice. Her long hair was up on her head fastened with a scrunchie, and she had on these awesome, long, silver bar earrings that I had never seen before. They sparkled whenever she moved her head. Plus, she had cute pink rhinestones in all the other earring holes.

Her dad popped open a beer really loud and pointed to the pizza box on the table. "You girls go ahead and eat."

"We're not hungry, Dad," Jenna said. Then she started giggling and put a hand up to her mouth because one of her Crest Strips was falling off.

I laughed, too. And we ran upstairs to her room.

"Oh my God! You got it!" I exclaimed.

Jenna pulled the strips off her teeth and picked up a beautiful red-and-black-striped top from her bed. She grinned like a spoiled brat. We'd seen that shirt together at the mall, at Abercrombie & Fitch, the week before, but it was so incredibly expensive none of us could afford it.

"Mom got it for me," Jenna said, waggling her eyebrows up and down.

"Oh, I hate you. I *love* that shirt!" I snatched it away from her and sat on the edge of her bed. No question I was envious. I'd been thinking of asking for that shirt for my birthday.

"Look what else she got me." Jenna picked up a small brown leather purse from her bureau. It wasn't a shoulder strap, but the kind lots of girls were carrying around now. It was cute.

She put the purse down and kind of bounced into a seat beside me on the bed. "So," she said, cocking her head, "do you want to hear what happened to Suzanne?"

I didn't even get a chance to answer.

"Girls! Come and eat!" Jenna's father hollered from the stairwell. He had a really loud voice, like a Marine sergeant or something. We jumped to our feet and scooted downstairs.

In the kitchen, we watched as her father tilted his head back and took a really long drink of beer. You could see his Adam's apple moving up and down when he swallowed. I wondered if he was going to chug the whole can at once. When he finished, he wiped his mouth with the back of his hand.

"Go ahead. Eat," he told us.

"But I don't want to yet," Jenna tried to tell him.

"*Eat!*" he ordered.

Something about the way he said it. Quickly, we pulled out stools at the kitchen counter and sat down. Jenna opened the pizza box, and each of us took a slice while her father walked into the family room and turned on the TV.

Jenna handed me a napkin, and I started picking pieces of mushroom off one piece of pizza. Even though I'd had that hot dog, I was still hungry. I was always hungry. But I just ate the mushrooms.

"So what did Suzanne's mother do?" I asked in a low voice.

"Um . . ." Jenna held up a finger—she had just polished her nails blue—because she had a mouthful. "You won't believe this." She swallowed and leaned toward me. *"Her mother is putting her in Catholic school."*

I sucked in my breath. "Are you serious?"

Jenna nodded, and the long silver earrings swung back and forth catching the light. "I'm not kidding you. I don't even think she's going to be at school tomorrow."

"You can do it that fast? Change schools?"

Jenna shrugged. "I guess. I told her she was nuts. I mean, she'll have to wear one of those dumb little kilts."

I put a hand to my mouth because I felt awful for Suzanne. She hated skirts.

Suddenly—incredibly—it was on the evening news! We could hear it! *A report about us!* About three girls at Oakdale Middle School telling officials what Mr. Mattero did. The reporter, a woman in this low-cut sweater, but with a really butch haircut, stood outside of our school, right beside the out-door sign that said PTO BOOK FAIR FRIDAY. She didn't say our names, she just said three girls had come forward and accused "Frederick Mattero, a music teacher at the school for the past eleven years . . ."

Jenna and I couldn't believe it. We slid off the stools and moved into the doorway to the family room, never taking our eyes off the television. I pulled on the ends of my braids. The reporter pointed to the front door of our school, like Mr. Mattero was going to come out or something. "It happened here, at Oakdale Middle School," the reporter said. "The teacher has been suspended with pay until an investigation is complete."

Jenna's dad blew the air out of his cheeks and belched. "Don't worry, that guy's gonna be sorry big-time for what he did," he muttered. He stomped back to the kitchen and popped open another can of beer.

We sat down on the couch together, Jenna and I. And that's when she started whimpering. "I wish Mommy was here. Can we call Mommy?"

Her father came out of the kitchen. "Yeah. Yeah, of course we can. We can call your mother. He frowned. "Where is she, you know? She in San Diego?"

Jenna shrugged. "You'll have to call the airline."

Her father slammed an address book onto the counter and flipped it open. He picked up the cell phone and punched in a number.

I watched Jenna. She had stopped whimpering instantly and was all eyes on her father. Behind Jenna, on the side table at the end of the couch, was a framed picture of her parents all dressed up for a party. Her mother was really beautiful. Thick blonde hair. Perfect skin. Really good makeup. Not to mention a perfect figure. Jenna was like a miniature version of her.

"Yeah, this is Bob Cartwright. I need to get in touch with my wife, Elaine. Elaine Cartwright. You know what flight she's working?"

Jenna and I couldn't hear what the airline was telling him. We only heard her father's side of the conversation.

"She's working—of course she's working. She left yesterday, and she's not due back until Friday . . . yeah, yeah, you're darn right, buddy, you'd better check again . . . What do you mean she's off until Sunday?"

Jenna's father flashed a look over at us. Jenna sat up. I heard her take a breath.

"Are you sure?" His eyes flashed, but his voice grew oddly quiet. "Yeah . . . I hear ya." He clicked off the phone, and, slowly, he settled it onto the counter. A lot of thoughts must have been racing through his mind.

In this incredibly calm voice, Jenna made a suggestion. "You could call Captain O'Brien. I bet he knows where Mommy is."

Her father narrowed his eyes at her. A really cold, hard stare that gave me the shivers. "O'Brien? What, that pilot?"

Jenna nodded, and honest to pete, you could see the red creeping into her dad's face.

Her father slammed the address book onto the counter and flipped it open again. He punched in more numbers and started marching back and forth in the kitchen. I sat there—stupid, naïve me, curious if that pilot guy knew where Jenna's mom might be since she wasn't working a flight like she'd told everyone.

"Yeah, hi," Jenna's father said into the phone as he turned his back on us. "This Tim O'Brien? This is Bob Cartwright. Look, there's, ah, been an emergency here with our daughter, Jenna, and I'm trying to find Elaine. You know where she's at? . . . Jenna's all right, yeah—well—well, actually, I don't know. They took her to the hospital, which is where I'm headed. Look, it's real important for me to find Elaine. If you have any idea . . . sure, yeah, sure I'll hold on . . ."

Jenna glanced at me and bit her bottom lip. She looked really scared.

Suddenly someone was back on the line with Jenna's dad. He walked away from us into the dining room with the cell phone at his ear. "Elaine? Is that you?" he asked. "What the hell are you doing at O'Brien's? *What the hell is going on?*"

At that point, we got up from the couch. Jenna started making her way down the hall toward the stairs to her room.

But I found my way out the door and ran all the way home.

Melody

I STAYED LATER THAN USUAL AT THE BARN, slowly measuring out grain and making sure each horse in each stall had three squares of hay. When there were no more chores, I returned to Nova's stall and gently clucked to her. She turned around, still munching on her hay, and came over to the door so I could stroke her nose and say good-bye.

It was dusk by the time I left, and I didn't want to cut through the pasture. Instead, I took the long way home: down the winding dirt driveway from the stables to a longer, gravel road, which led back to the main road and our neighborhood. But even then, I scuffed along, wanting more time to think, but not knowing what to think, and so mostly torturing myself with thoughts of the worst that could happen: the school firing Dad, the police putting him in jail. I did not actually think these things would happen, understand, I was just doing worst-case scenarios in my head.

By the time I crested the hill on Bellevue Avenue, it was dark.

I saw that my brother was home ahead of me. His car, a beat-up Toyota my grandmother gave him, was parked on the street out front, its windows down and one tire looking mighty soft. Sometimes Cade worked after school at a video store and didn't get home until almost nine, but I could never keep track of his schedule.

Seeing the soft yellow lights on inside the kitchen window, I figured Cade knew by now, too. He had a pretty quick temper; I wondered how he was taking the news.

I plucked the evening paper out of the azalea bushes, where it had been tossed, and walked in to see my family sitting around the kitchen table with several Chinese food takeout cartons, unopened, in front of them. Cade was frowning and had picked up a wooden chopstick, which he slowly tapped on the open palm of one hand.

No one seemed to notice me. Dad was staring at the edge of the table.

"The school has a policy, Cade," Mom was explaining quietly, opening her folded hands in front of her. "Anytime a teacher is accused of anything, not just touching a student, that teacher has to be put on leave while the allegations are investigated."

"Who's investigating him?" Cade asked.

"The school, the police. A detective called a while ago and asked if Dad would go down to the station and answer a few questions tomorrow."

Cade rolled his eyes. "So how long will he have to stay out of work?"

"I don't know," Mom said.

"And what about the girls who accused him?" Cade demanded. "They're a bunch of liars! So they just go to school? Like nothing happened?"

Neither one of my parents responded right away. Dad lifted his head. "There's nothing else we can do right now."

When Cade brought his two hands down, I thought he was going to break that chopstick in half.

"We just have to wait and see what happens," my mother continued. "Your father wrote a statement denying everything. I'm going to drop it off with Mrs. Fernandez tomorrow morning."

Cade threw the chopstick down and leaned back in his chair. Angrily crossing his arms, he looked at Dad. "That's it? You're just going to stand by and let those kids call you a pedophile?"

"That's enough, Cade!" my mother yelled, breaking her calm facade. "Stop it right now, do you hear?"

"Mary!" my dad stopped her. "Take it easy."

The room fell quiet. Mom covered her face with her hands. She hates to yell. It absolutely takes everything out of her when she yells.

Even knowing this, in the vacuum of silence following her outburst, I dared to ask: "What's a pedophile?" I had an idea, but I wasn't sure.

Surprised, they turned to look at me. Mom uncovered her face, and Cade uncrossed his arms. His eyes flicked from Mom and then to Dad, who got up and left.

"A pedophile," Mom explained, her voice flat, "is somebody who abuses children."

It was an awful night. None of us even ate dinner. I was the one who opened, then closed, those little cartons of Chinese food and stacked them in the refrigerator. While Mom and Dad sat quietly in the family room, I fed the cat, took the garbage out, and wiped off the counters. After that, I couldn't think of anything else I could do to help, so I stood in the doorway watching them watch each other. Finally, Mom noticed me and said, "Mellie, do you have homework?"

I nodded and left. I had some sentences in Spanish to translate, an English grammar quiz to study for, and some reading in social studies. Up in my room I undid my long braid, took a shower, and changed into pajamas. Then I piled the books I needed on my bed and sat cross-legged behind them. Harmony jumped up and nuzzled my elbow, then laid across my open Spanish book. I let her stay.

"I forgot," Mom said a few minutes later, after sticking her head in my bedroom door. "Annie called while you were at the stables. She said to call back, that she would be home all evening."

"Thanks," I told her. I had promised Annie I'd call. And anyway, we always touched base sometime after school. Lots of times we studied over the phone or online. But I didn't even want to talk to my best friend. I didn't want to have to explain what had happened. In part because I really didn't know. I didn't feel as though I had all the facts.

I opened my grammar book, but my eyes glazed over and I ended up examining the bottom of my foot, picking at a piece of dead skin.

"Oh, and by the way, Melody," Mom said, startling me when she reappeared. "We all talked about it before you got home. We decided that if Song calls from the university, we won't say anything. She's working on a term paper that's due next week, and this would be terribly distracting."

"Okay," I agreed, although it seemed a little unfair to me that Song wouldn't have to worry like the rest of us.

I propped up the pillows behind me, pulled out the folded grammar worksheet that needed to be finished, then read and reread the instructions several times: *Circle the correct pronoun and describe its function in the sentence.* But my mind kept wandering, composing its own sentences. *The girls made up a story to get* him *in trouble.* He *was surprised when* they *reported* him *to the principal.* Social studies. I'd try social studies instead. But after lifting and positioning the heavy book on my lap, I couldn't even open it.

Instead, I looked around my room. At my bookshelf full of horse statues and horse books. At my stuffed animals piled high in a net sling in the corner of my room. At the bureau where I stood every morning brushing and braiding my long hair. At the picture of my family on the wall beside the bureau, a picture taken the morning we played for everyone at church. I liked the picture because we were all holding our instruments, and we had big smiles and our arms wrapped around one another.

My eyes drifted downward, to the viola case propped against the side of my desk, notebooks and music piled beside it. I wrinkled my nose. It was a secret that I didn't like playing viola. I only did it for my parents, especially Dad, because he wanted me to be part of the orchestra at school. I felt guilty about it because I knew how much my parents wanted me to play an instrument, like them—and like Song, who was so good on both the flute and the piano. I tried. I really did. But after flute, after clarinet, after viola, it hadn't clicked. I didn't *love* it the way Dad wanted me to love it. I felt so bad about it, but I was hoping by the time I got to high school, I could tell Dad the truth. I wanted to drop the music so I could put more time into the lit magazine and horseback riding.

But even that little secret seemed so trivial now, in the light of what had happened. In just a few hours, everything seemed different, even though nothing, really, had changed.

The phone rang downstairs. I got up off my bed and went to the upstairs hallway to listen. "It's on TV?" I heard Mom say.

But no one in our house turned the television on that night.

Still, there was no escaping from it. In the morning, a story appeared in the newspaper: MIDDLE SCHOOL MUSIC TEACHER ACCUSED OF SEXUAL ABUSE. The article said my father—Frederick Mattero, the music teacher at Oakdale Middle School—had been placed on administrative leave after three students accused him of sexual abuse. The article didn't say that Dad denied it—or that the girls might have lied. It only said there was an investigation.

"It feels like someone kicked me in the stomach," Cade complained.

Mom was quiet and walked around, setting bowls on the table, pouring cereal and juice and trying to get us to eat.

Dad sat looking stunned, in a chair at the table. The puffy redness around his eye had turned black and blue overnight.

"You ought to sue the guy who hit you," I told him, feeling the anger rise up again. When Dad didn't respond, I turned to Mom. "Really, why don't they arrest that guy for assault or something?"

Mom raised her eyebrows. "You're right." She turned to Dad. "Fred, we should ask about that."

Cade still frowned at the newspaper. "What am I supposed to tell people today?"

Like *he* was the only one who had to worry.

When his question went unanswered, he scraped his chair back and left abruptly, grabbing his books and his car keys from the counter, not even saying good-bye. It was so typical of my brother. He is so centered on himself.

The door slammed. Mom rushed after him. "Cade, are you working after school today? Cade?"

Dad still sat at the table. His elbows were on the table, and he had dropped his head into his hands so I couldn't see his face. He hadn't eaten, hadn't said a thing.

It was really strange going to school without Dad. For the last three years we had gone to school together, leaving the house at exactly seven-thirty A.M. so we would be there at seven forty-five, fifteen minutes before morning announcements, time for Dad to unlock the music room, turn the lights on, and get ready for class.

"Melody, are you ready?" Mom asked, scooping up her purse from the counter and settling the thin strap over her shoulder. She had on her work clothes: white sneakers, khaki pants, a green polo shirt with the words GREENTHUMB NURSERY embossed on the front. Mom's job kept her in good shape, and she always seemed so perky with her short brown hair curled under and tucked behind her ears, her little diamond studs sparkling in her ears.

"I'm ready," I replied.

Mom had in her hand a letter my father had written. I assumed he had denied touching any of those seventh-grade girls. She was taking it into the main office at school when she dropped me off.

She looked over at Dad, who by that time had gotten up

from the table and stood nearby in his bathrobe, a cup of coffee in his hands.

"Are you going to the police station?" she asked him. "To talk with that detective?"

Dad nodded.

"And what about the lie–detector test?" she asked.

Dad shrugged. He seemed lost. "I don't know," he said, glancing at me, then settling his eyes on Mom.

"Fred, look," Mom told him, "if you're at all nervous, don't do it, because the anxiety will skew the results and do more damage than good. Those tests, you know they're not perfect."

"Yeah, well, neither am I."

I frowned, wondering what he meant by that. Mom stared at him.

"Well, for crying out loud, Mary," Dad snapped. "How's it going to look if I refuse to take the lie detector?"

Bad. It would look bad. We all knew the answer to that one.

"Here, Mellie, you'd better deliver this," Dad said, picking up his familiar blue planning book from the table and handing it to me. "I wrote out what we're supposed to do today. Seventh-graders are practicing their recorders. Eighth grade is having an open–note quiz on the concert band."

"Who should I give it to?" I asked.

"Just put it on my desk," Dad said.

Suddenly, Mom had her purse off her shoulder and was scooping up the unfinished bowls of cereal.

"Stop, Mary," Dad told her, trying to take a dish from her hands. "I'll do that, I'll clean up."

Mom put the dish in the sink.

Dad touched her wrist. "What else am I going to do today?"

Mom picked up her car keys again. "I do have to get going, Fred. I've got a huge shipment of impatiens coming this morning. *Huge.* And all that mulch. And I'm short one person because of Martha being sick."

"Go," Dad ordered.

But Mom began to cry.

Dad put his arms around her. "Come on, Mary," Dad said softly. "You need to hold yourself together. For *me*—for all of us. You have to, or we won't get through this."

(11) Claire

WHEN THE ALARM WENT OFF IN THE MORNING, I woke up with a rotten feeling. Kind of like hunger, only worse.

"Claire, time to get up," Mom called sweetly.

Remembering why I felt so bad, I moaned and curled up into a ball, then stuck my hand out and pulled the blanket up over my shoulder. I could have stayed that way all day. I even thought about telling Mom I didn't feel good, that I had, like, a sore throat or something. But I also wanted to find out what would happen at school. And I wanted to hear what went down with Jenna's mom and dad after I ran home the night before.

My eyes flicked open. I hadn't even told my mother I went to Jenna's. See, when I got home, Mom and the kids weren't back yet, so I destroyed the note I'd left on the counter. Why upset my mother any more? She didn't want me with Jenna, and she'd go ballistic if she found out about Jenna's mother being at that pilot's house. She'd probably never let me back over Jenna's again.

And yet it did all seem kind of strange. I rolled over on my back and put my hands up behind my head, thinking. I kept playing that scene over and over in my mind—how Jenna whimpered and asked for her mother. "Let's call the airline. Maybe Captain O'Brien knows where Mommy is . . ." I mean, did Jenna know all along where her mother was? Did she plan that?

I wondered if Jenna's parents would get divorced now. If that happened, then Jenna might have to move. It seemed like kids always had to move when their parents got divorced. And if Suzanne went to Catholic school—then I'd be all alone at Oakdale.

"Claire, come on, honey!" Mom called again, a little louder.

I pushed off the covers and hauled myself out of bed. Pulled up my sweatpants that were falling off and padded down the dark hall in my socks. The door to Corky and Izzy's room was open, and in the dim pinkish light thrown by the cow-jumping-over-the-moon night-light, I could see a lump under the cowboy quilt that was Corky and how Izzy slept with one foot up against the side of her crib. Not very ladylike. I had to smile a little at that. All over again, I wished I could just stay home. Play games with Corky and Izzy. Read them stories and take them down to the playground. Anything to avoid all the crap I was surely headed for at school.

Reluctantly I moved down the unlit stairs, one hand against the wall to guide me. I could smell coffee before I got to the kitchen, where Dad was sitting at the table reading the newspaper and Mom was standing at the counter, mixing waffle batter.

They looked up when I walked in.

"You okay this morning?" Dad asked. He'd been pretty upset the night before when I told him what Mr. Mattero did, even though he didn't go nuts, like Jenna's father. Generally, my dad is pretty level-headed. Even with all of Corky's problems, his food allergies, his autism, Dad didn't get all bent out of shape the way Mom sometimes did.

"Mattero. Who is this guy?" Dad had asked after Corky and Izzy had been put to bed. We let him eat the supper Mom had kept for him in the microwave before breaking the news to him. Then we talked about it while we all cleaned up, Mom doing the dishes, Dad drying the pots, and me putting the rest of the food away.

"He's my music teacher," I told him.

"Mattero. Mattero. It's familiar. Wasn't there a piece in the paper a little while back, about the band at your school going to some big contest that they've won for like nine years straight?"

"Probably," I said.

"I think so. I think that's the guy," Dad had decided. He leaned in close to Mom and took a wet skillet from her soapy, gloved hands. "Makes you wonder, doesn't it?" he asked her, "what that slime bag was doing on all those band trips out of town."

———

Mom waved a spatula at me. "Claire, honey, you don't look like you're awake yet."

I guess I must have been standing there in the kitchen like a zombie.

"You okay?" Dad repeated, more intently. He was already dressed for work, with a tie and everything—even though it seemed like he just got home.

"Yeah. I'm all right," I said, pulling out a chair at the kitchen table and squinting from the overhead light. But that wasn't exactly the truth because I wasn't all right. I was worried about what happened at Jenna's house, and I wasn't feeling so good about us telling Mrs. Fernandez what Mr. Mattero did. I mean, maybe we just shouldn't have said anything because now Suzanne had to go to another school.

I sat cross-legged on the chair and checked out the fingernail on my left hand. It was still sore, and you could tell I'd bitten down on it too far again. I curled my fingers around it and then pulled over my hands the long sleeves of the oversized T-shirt I'd slept in.

Usually, there was something nice about being up this early with my parents, which was the only time I had them both to myself. But that morning, I felt mixed up—and a little scared.

Mom set a plate in front of me.

I groaned. "Mom, you *know* I don't want waffles." Not just because waffles are fattening, but because the quinoa waffles she made always gave me a stomachache. I think because of the sparkling water she used to make them. She had to though; Corky was allergic to yeast.

Just then I realized the little braids I wore to bed would make my hair superwavy. No way was I going to school like that. Not even a few squirts of that antifrizz stuff was going to save me.

"I need a shower," I announced. "I'll take, like, a yogurt with me." Yogurt wasn't bad. Only like a hundred and twenty calories, the low-fat kind.

Mom had long ago given up arguing with me over food. Which was good. She handed me a cherry vanilla and a spoon.

On the bus, the kids were buzzing with gossip about what Mr. Mattero did, the fact that he wouldn't be there, and guesses about who the three girls were who reported him.

"Did you see it on the news?"

"It was in the newspaper, too."

"My father says he's not allowed at school anymore . . ."

"I'll bet one of those girls is Mandy. Yeah, she's such a slut. That one with the green hair?"

Suzanne wasn't on the bus that morning, only Jenna. But we didn't sit together. We never do in the morning. Bus is too crowded after my stop, and she gets on two stops later. I didn't talk to anyone. I spent the entire bus ride scraping the rest of the purple nail polish off my fingernails with the top of a Bic pen and thinking about Suzanne, how she would have to wear a kilt and go to Catholic school. She was so shy, and with her inhaler and her braces and her so-so complexion and all, it would take her years to make a new friend. And just when us three had such a good thing going.

Poor Suzanne, I thought, shaking my head. It didn't seem fair. *She* was the one who didn't want to say anything. "It'll just get us in trouble," she kept warning in her whiny voice. But Jenna had already decided we had to say something. I rolled my eyes. I mean, I loved Jenna. She was cool and fun and all that, but I really had to wonder what it was going to be like, just her and me at Oakdale.

At school, Jenna caught up to me in the hallway. But even then, with the noise of slamming lockers, whoops, laughs, and bits of conversation, I kept hearing those same questions. *"Do you know who it is?" "What did he do?" "Did you see it on the news?"*

I was surprised, but Jenna seemed like she was in a good mood. Her lips kind of curled up, and she was looking around. Like it was cool to have everyone talking about us.

"Hey there," she finally said to me.

We walked a ways. "What happened after I left last night?" I asked her. "I mean with your dad?"

Jenna's good mood took a dive. "Oh, man," she moaned. "My father was really, *really* mad."

We stopped, and when I looked at Jenna close-up, I could see that she had dark smudges under her eyes, like she hadn't washed off her mascara. But she had on those same silver bar and rhinestone earrings, which were really pretty, and her hair was wrapped up, secured in a giant tortoiseshell clip, and she had on some kind of new pink lipstick. I felt my heart drop a little. Even when Jenna was tired, she looked great.

"My mom's coming home today," Jenna said in a low voice, but I don't know why because no one was listening. "My parents are gonna talk. But don't tell anyone, okay, Claire? Don't tell anyone about what happened last night. Do you promise?"

I nodded. "Sure." The great thing about us three is that we could trust each other with stuff we said. Suddenly, I realized I needed to put an elastic in my damp hair. "Will you hold these books for a minute?"

After Jenna took the books, I raked my fingers back through my hair to make a ponytail.

"I knew my mom was at that guy's house last night," Jenna went on.

"You did?"

"Yeah. She's been seeing him for months. And *he's* married, too!"

I studied her while I pulled my hair through the elastic. She really looked disgusted. I was surprised she hadn't told us about that guy before.

"He sounds like a real loser," I said, reaching into my sweat-shirt pocket to get two barrettes, which I snapped in place on either side of my head, to hold back my growing-out bangs. I was also thinking that Jenna's mom was partly to blame for this, too, but I didn't say that out loud.

Jenna grew angrier. "Yeah. He's a freak. I *hate* him! And I don't want him to break up my family!"

I took my books back. "Then you did the right thing, Jenna," I sympathized. "I mean, your dad had to know sooner or later, right?"

We never got beyond that because just then we saw some girls pointing at us, and Sabrina Coster, this eighth-grader we know from our old school, came over. "It was you guys, wasn't it?" she demanded. "My friend, Stefanie, she said she saw you in the office yesterday with Mrs. Fernandez."

My eyes flicked to Jenna. What did she think? Because it wasn't clear whose side Sabrina was on. Her voice had a nasty edge to it.

Jenna lifted her chin. "Yeah, it was us," she acknowledged. I'm telling you, Jenna is not afraid of anyone. "It was a bad thing what Mr. Mattero did."

Sabrina narrowed her eyes. "We're going to miss the band competition next week now. We've been working for it all year."

Jenna widened her eyes at me, as though to say, Do you believe this?

"We may not even get our money back if we don't go," Sabrina said.

Jenna turned on her. "Well, what do you want *me* to do about it?"

A couple of other kids had stopped to listen.

"It was *you*?" one of the boys asked Jenna.

Jenna flashed her eyes at him but didn't say anything.

The boy came closer and smiled at her. "Man, you had a lot of guts to go in there and tell Fernandez."

"What did he do?" another girl interrupted after pushing her way through the crowd. I recognized that girl from my gym class. "What did Mattero do?"

Jenna's head swung from the boy to the girl and then back to the boy.

"He's weird," another girl piped up. "One time, he gave me a detention for, like, nothing, and I had to stay after school. Just him and me in the band room."

"Yeah, and once me and Kristen were in there practicing flute," another joined in, "and he asked us to stay and help him clean up. We didn't though. Uh–uh. I remember—I had to go to my brother's wrestling match."

While they were all putting in their two cents' worth, I stepped back from the crowd while keeping an eye on that girl, Sabrina. She fixed her cold little beady eyes on me, too, and kept staring, even after she got pushed to the edge of the crowd. I lost sight of her, but then the next thing you know she was, like, right in my face. "I think you're a bunch of liars," she accused icily.

I spun away from her and walked off. Fast. I glanced back

once, and she was still staring at me. Ugh. It gave me the creeps.
I mean, what did she want from me?

And did other people hear her?

In music class that day, there was a substitute teacher. A real
ding-a-ling. We'd had her before. She's sort of fat, and she wore
these loose brown old-lady pants and an oversized blouse that
pulled so tight across her chest it popped open between the but-
tons. She was so gross. Even her hair—it looked like it just came
off a set of rollers and she forgot to brush it. She was sipping a
Coke and had an opened package of Fritos on her desk, which
you could smell and which reminded me how hungry I was.

"Get out your recorders," Mrs. Fatso said. She must have said
it ten times, but never very loud, which is why no one was listening to her.

"Get out your recorders!" she finally yelled.

So we took our recorders out of their blue leather cases. A
kid in my class, Aaron Brown, started playing "Yankee Doodle
Dandy," and we laughed.

Spencer Leigh, behind me, had a lion puppet on his hand
and pulled my ponytail. He growled when I turned around.

And that's what music class was like that day.

No one seemed to miss Mr. Mattero. We were so incredibly
bored in his class. I can't even remember what we were studying—major and minor modes. Dynamics. Texture. Stuff like
that. Oh yeah, and music where one voice has the melody,

called homophony. Only Mr. Mattero had wrote it on the board
before he pronounced it, and Travis Gilmore called out he had
nothing against gay people and Mr. Mattero shouldn't be making fun of them. We all bust a gut laughing that day. *"Hoh-MAH-*
foh-nee, not homophobic!" poor Mr. Mattero tried to explain. I don't
think he ever did get control of our class after that.

During music I doodled inside the cover of my music notebook. Flowers, faces, long swirlie doodads. The kids should
have been on their knees with gratitude for what Jenna,
Suzanne, and I did.

The sub was pathetic. She didn't know squat about the
recorder. Which, by the way, I could play "Ode to Joy" on, like,
perfect. It's the first instrument I've ever played, too. When we
blew into our instruments, we all played different songs.

"Stop! Stop the music!" the sub hollered. Now that I think of
it, it was the last time all year we ever touched those recorders.
Too bad, because we were going to play them in the spring
concert. Mom was going to bring Corky and Izzy. And my
grandmother even said she would come, to hear me play.

Word got around fast. At lunch, it was pretty obvious that
everyone in school knew it was us who had told on Mr. Mattero. Everybody was whispering and pointing. Some other kids
came right out and asked us. When we didn't answer, a teacher
nearby told everybody to mind their own business.

At lunch, Jenna and I sat together, near a group of seventh-grade goody-goodies who made you want to puke. One of them, this girl, Emily, said to us, "It took a lot of courage to go in and report what Mr. Mattero did."

Jenna snorted a little. She can't stand that group.

But really, it was a nice thing to say to us.

"Thanks," I told her, good and loud so Jenna could hear. "We really appreciate it."

Still, we didn't strike up any more of a conversation with them or anything. We went back to eating, which for Jenna was a hot lunch: lasagna, green beans, a roll with butter, and sliced, canned peaches. It looked delicious. Me, I had an old chocolate cherry Luna bar—smashed—that I'd found in the bottom of my backpack because I forgot to pack an apple. I had money, sure. My mother gave me lunch money every day. But eating lunch is a total waste of calories, and besides, that's where I got money for clothes and stuff. So a Luna and a bottle of water. I probably should have skipped lunch, but that day we ate late with eighth grade, and I was absolutely starving.

Suddenly, there was this food fight in another corner of the cafeteria. We heard kids laughing and saw some boys stand up to throw something. Then a girl sprang up out of her chair and ran from the cafeteria.

I heard one of the seventh-graders near us lean forward into her group and say, "That's Melody. Yeah. That's Mr. Mattero's daughter."

(12) Melody

"IS IT TRUE WHAT THEY SAID ABOUT YOUR DAD?"

"Who reported him?"

"Do you know who told?"

"Is he in, like, big trouble?"

The questions pummeled me as soon as I got to school. Mom had given me a quick hug and headed to the office to deliver Dad's letter, but my locker was in the opposite direction. I had to go on alone, shouldering my way through the thick and boisterous morning crowd, teeth clenched, stomach in a knot, ignoring every question and comment that came in my direction. *Kept* coming in my direction, even as I spun the dial on my locker trying to find the right numbers, but kept missing and so had to keep spinning.

Thank God for Annie. She is everything a best friend could be. As soon as she saw my hunched shoulders and the tears creeping into my eyes, she took over.

"Beat it!" she hollered at everyone clustered around me. She

even waved her arm around as though threatening to smack anyone who got too close. "It's not Melody's fault! Leave her alone!"

People backed off.

"Bunch of animals," Annie muttered, her eyes sweeping the hallway, on the lookout for anyone even thinking about coming toward us. "They're like vultures, aren't they? Disgusting vultures!"

I flipped my braid back over my shoulder, and I might have laughed at Annie's reaction if I wasn't trying so hard not to cry.

"Hey, are you okay?" Annie asked, bending her head close to mine. She had a burst of curly, frizzy black hair that seemed extra wild that morning.

"Yeah. I'm okay. I just didn't know what to say to anyone."

"God, it's awful, Melody. We saw it on the news last night and in the paper this morning. How come you didn't call me?"

"I couldn't. I didn't know what to tell you."

"Do you know who those girls are?" she asked. It was the same question everyone else had asked, but Annie wanting to know was different.

"I know one's named Jenna somebody. Dad said the other names but they weren't familiar. Oh, there's a Claire—I *think*. They're seventh-graders."

"Seventh grade! That is *such* a creepy class. A total bunch of losers."

I felt better now with Annie beside me, verbally bashing the entire seventh grade because of what three girls had done. I pushed my glasses back up on my nose and went back to the combination on my locker, finally finding the right numbers. Metal clicked. My locker opened. "Thanks," I told her.

"Sure." She scanned the hallway again. "Get your stuff and let's go."

We headed to homeroom, but first, I had to stop in the music room to drop off my father's planner so the substitute would know what to do. It was painful opening his door. No one had arrived yet; the room was dark.

I flipped the switch, and, as the lights flickered on above the carpeted, tiered steps of the rehearsal room, I walked over to my father's desk. As usual, it was a mess. Piles of music books. The CDs we'd stacked up the day before. A copy of *Great Songs of the 60s* beside a tape of Vivaldi's *Four Seasons*. A container of keyboard cleaner. A vial of clear slide oil for the trombones. And among the scattered pens, pencil halves, and assorted pieces of paper, an open can of Diet Coke.

Setting my backpack on the floor, I took a minute to straighten up, quickly making separate piles of books, music, and other things. I placed the can of soda in the wastebasket and when I finally had a clear space on his desk, I retrieved Dad's day planner from my backpack and set it down. I even opened it up to the right day so the substitute would see what Dad had planned.

"Come *on*," Annie beckoned from the doorway.

I scooped up my backpack, but on the way out I paused to look at the notice on his bulletin board for the upcoming competition in Virginia. There was a picture of the amusement park where we would all spend the day after the contest at Patrick Henry High School in Ashland. And a brochure of the hotel where we were staying. It had an indoor pool, a game room with video machines, and a restaurant where we could order what we wanted because we'd be bringing our own meal money.

EVERYONE SHOULD BE PRACTICING AT LEAST ONE HOUR A DAY.

My father's note on a piece of white paper was printed by hand, each word underlined.

I wondered how long it would take the police to do an investigation. Would they get it done in time for us to have a final rehearsal and go to the competition the week after next? What if they didn't get it done in time? Would Dad have to cancel the trip? Could the school let him do that after all the work we'd done? All the money we'd raised at bake sales? At car washes?

"Hurry up!" Annie called in. And it suddenly struck me as odd—really odd—that Annie hadn't even set foot in the room.

After going to English together, Annie and I had to split up for different classes, her to Spanish and me to social studies.

None of my good friends were in that class with me, and I was not prepared, so I leaned over my desk, resting my forehead against my hand and hoping it looked as though I had a headache. My history teacher, Mr. Woburn, was pretty cool; I hoped he would understand and not call on me.

Discussion centered on World War II, which was our reading the night before. "How did the Allies force Germany and Japan to surrender?" Mr. Woburn asked. Hands went up, but not mine. While they discussed the answer, I drifted into my own thoughts, wondering how Mom was doing while she arranged all those impatiens at the nursery, and how Cade was surviving at the high school.

I worried about Dad and tried to imagine what questions the detective would be asking him for the lie–detector test. I did not doubt that my father would pass that test. Why *wouldn't* he? All he had to do was answer simple, basic questions and tell the truth of what happened. Questions that Detective Daniels said he would even know beforehand.

And just at that moment I had an incredibly random thought. I thought about my viola. I saw it in my mind, leaning in its case against my desk, and how, out of a sense of duty, I took it out and practiced for half an hour five days a week. I was good at fooling my parents. They didn't have a clue what a chore it was. Could a lie–detector test expose *me*?

Melody Mattero, do you enjoy playing your viola?

Oh, absolutely! Of course I do!

How deep down did a secret have to be before it was completely safe? And if there was a safe zone, then how could you ever really be sure that anyone was telling the truth? Even my father! What if Dad had lied about not touching those girls? What if he really did do something and was so ashamed he didn't want to tell us?

Startled, I sat up abruptly. I could not believe those thoughts had the audacity to come into my mind!

Mr. Woburn must have figured I had the answer to his question.

"Melody?"

I blinked and stared at him.

"Why was penicillin so important during World War II?" he repeated.

Penicillin? I bit my lip and frowned, making it look as though I was trying hard to remember. *What was penicillin? A person? A legal term? No, it was a medical thing, some kind of—*

"Did you do the reading last night?" he asked.

"Yes," I said instantly, afraid to tell him I hadn't. But didn't Mr. Woburn know what happened to my dad? How could he call on me like this? He started looking around the room, to ask someone else I assumed, which would have only humiliated me more.

"Penicillin was important," I began.

"Yes?" Mr. Woburn looked over his glasses at me.

"Because it saved lives?" I guessed.

"Excellent! It saved lives." Mr. Woburn lifted his head, tapped a piece of chalk against his palm, and walked down the aisle behind my desk. "Remember that during World War I, fifteen percent of all soldiers who died had succumbed to infection."

I sighed with relief, closed my eyes, and slumped back against my chair.

Annie was waiting for me in the hallway after social studies. We were scheduled for a study hall together the next period and had passes written out enabling us to go to the library, where we planned to make a recruiting poster for the literary magazine. Mrs. Humphries, our club adviser, had suggested we make a list of ten reasons to join. So far we'd come up with only two:

1. It's a great way for you to show off your writing skills!

2. It's a great way for you to improve your writing skills!

During study hall Annie thought of three more:

3. You'll learn responsibility!

4. You might make a new friend!

5. It's cool to see your name in print!

"Look," I said, "I don't think we need to use so many exclamation points."

"But we have to make it sound exciting," Annie argued.

I thought about that. "Why don't we just say there will be free snacks?"

Annie lit up. "Great idea! We'll do that *and* the exclamation points!"

I rolled my eyes; she laughed. But we made it to six. After that, we couldn't think of anything else.

"Let's finish when you come over tomorrow night," I said.

"Okay," she said. "We can be thinking of things in the mean-time."

I agreed. Then Annie took out her poem to work on for the rest of the period, and I did the same, only all I did was doodle in the margins.

Annie and I were part of a larger group at school. A group that included Jane, Jean, Noelle, Lucy, and Liz. We were in a lot of honors classes together. We were in chorus, orchestra, or band. And in the fall we were all on the field hockey team for Oak-dale. In the spring, we did different things, some of us lacrosse, some of us tennis. Annie and I didn't even do a spring sport because we worked on the literary magazine. But every day, no fail, we ate lunch together at the long table by the double doors that led outside.

That day was no different. We met in the cafeteria, saved seats by throwing down backpacks and sweatshirts, and those of us getting hot lunch rushed to get in line.

No one in my group pestered me with questions about Dad, but I thought about him as I pushed my tray along in the food line. My father always brought his lunch to school and ate at his desk, using the extra time to repair instruments or grade papers.

A square of lasagna and a big spoonful of string beans were dished out onto a plate and slid over the counter to me. A weird combination, I thought. But it didn't much matter. I wasn't very hungry. I took a roll, some sliced peaches, and a milk.

Walking back toward our table, I saw Noelle rushing toward me. She grabbed my elbow and whispered in my ear. "Mellie, we know who the girls are—those seventh-graders—two of them are eating lunch over there."

"Where?"

"*There,* by the windows," Noelle said. "Don't *look*! Just walk by. Second table from the right. The two at the end. One of them has blonde hair, see? With the streaks in it? The other one has brown hair—in a ponytail."

I walked by, but not very slowly because I was nervous. I glanced quickly but didn't recognize the ponytailed girl at all. Her face looked pinched. She was eating some sort of a granola bar. Another quick glance at the blonde, however, and I had a flash of recognition. But I couldn't quite place her.

Noelle was still beside me. "Do you know them?"

I shook my head. "Are you sure those are the girls?"

"Positive."

After we sat down, I started buttering my roll, but I kept looking over at the two girls.

"The blonde one's Jenna," said Liz, crouching beside me. "The other one is Claire. And one of them isn't in school today. Her name's Suzanne."

"How do you know that?"

Liz nodded toward Jane. "Jane's brother, Colin, is in seventh grade. He says everyone knows."

Annie settled her tray beside mine and pulled out the chair. "Do you want me to go over there and accidentally spill my lunch on them?" she asked. "Or my milk? I'm good with milk."

I smiled at her but shook my head. And vaguely, I heard some boys laughing at the table behind us. I heard the name "Mattero" and the word "bra." And very clearly, I heard the word "pervert" before a slimy string bean hit the side of my face. An explosion of laughter from the boys.

Pushing back my chair, I fled from the room.

Claire

I WAS BACK TO BITING MY THUMBNAIL so badly that my finger started bleeding again. It stung, too. I took a Kleenex from my backpack and wrapped it around the top part of my thumb. Then I kind of made a fist so you couldn't see it. There were only a few minutes to go in the last period of the day. Literature. Mrs. Sidley passed out paperback copies of the next book we were reading, *The Outsiders*. I might actually read this book, I thought, since I sort of felt like an outsider myself. I wondered if that was what the book was about, not fitting in. This year, even with Jenna, it didn't feel like we "fit in" so much as we had just carved out our own little world and had each other.

"One other handout!" Mrs. Sidley announced. She gave it to us as we walked out the door. A sheet of paper with Oakdale Middle School at the top and Mrs. Fernandez's signature at the bottom:

Dear Students, Parents, and Staff:

I want to inform you of a serious incident within our school that

has had terrible consequences for several of our students and their
families, as well as a member of our staff . . .

I knew that note was about us—Jenna, Suzanne, and me—
and I didn't want to read it. In all the hustle and bustle of the
final bell, when kids were pushing through the doorway, I
crumpled up the letter and dropped it in a wastebasket.

On the already-crowded bus, I could see that Jenna was saving me a seat toward the back. It felt like everybody watched
me as I turned sideways to squeeze myself down the aisle. They
all knew it was us now. I didn't like the attention. Why were
they making such a big deal out of it anyway? I almost didn't
want to sit with Jenna because of what was happening, but she
patted the spot beside her and scooted over, so I sat down.

We didn't talk to each other at first. Just waited until the bus
was full and jerked forward. That's when I leaned over toward
her and said in her ear: "I didn't know Mr. Mattero had a
daughter at our school."

Jenna shook her head a little. "No, I didn't either."

We hadn't had time to talk about it earlier.

I sighed because I felt bad for Melody Mattero. "Those kids
that threw the food at her were mean."

"What?"

You can't hear a darn thing on that bus without yelling.
"Those kids—they were mean!"

"Yeah," she agreed, but she was fiddling around with her

new charm bracelet, and I couldn't see her face, to see if she really meant it.

She used both hands to pull her long hair back over her shoulders. The bus bounced down the highway. A wad of paper hit me on the back of my head. I turned around to see who threw it, and so many kids laughed you couldn't tell.

At the first stop, some of the worst kids in the back got off. I was glad.

I readjusted the Kleenex on my thumb, which had stopped bleeding but still hurt.

Jenna turned to me when the bus moved again. "So what?"

"So what?" I repeated. Like what was she talking about?

"Yeah. Like so what if Mr. Mattero has a daughter?"

I just stared at her. Talk about a delayed reaction, I thought.

Jenna started examining her fingernails, but she knew I was looking at her. Suddenly, she flashed me this icy look and arched her eyebrows. "Maybe he abuses her, too," she said.

Something inside of me tightened up then. Tightened right up into a hard knot. And as the bus rolled on, that knot got bigger and bigger. I started adding things up in my head: Suzanne was not in school. The police were doing an investigation. Mr. Mattero had a daughter.

The next thing you know, Jenna had those silver earrings out of her earlobes and was handing them to me. "Here," she offered. "I know how much you like them."

It was so random! I couldn't believe it. I loved those earrings. "Are you sure? I mean, why?"

Jenna smiled sweetly. "'Cause we're best friends is why."

At the bus stop, after we got off, I asked her again, "Are you sure?"

But she just pushed my hand away. "Totally. They're yours."

I admired the shiny earrings in the palm of my hand. I thought it was really nice—and very generous—of Jenna to give those earrings to me.

"Good luck with your mom," I told her.

"Oh, yeah." She rolled her eyes. "Thanks."

Then we turned away from each other. Jenna went one way, and I went the other.

At our house, Mom was outside, washing our van. She turned off the hose when she saw me.

"Hi. How was school?"

I swung the backpack off my shoulder. "Okay, I guess."

"Anybody say anything? About the situation?"

"No, not really."

"Claire, are you all right?"

"Yeah, I'm all right." I kind of snapped the words at her because I didn't feel like talking about it, and my mom is always trying to get stuff out of me. "I'm just hungry," I told her, scrunching up my nose.

"Well, you know what there is. Yogurt, cheese—apples, some

new apples. When you go in, be quiet, okay? Both the kids are napping."

Inside, I dropped my backpack on the floor, went straight up to my room, and closed the door. My stomach was rattling because I'd only had the Luna bar for lunch. I fell on my bed, picked up my platypus, and lay it on my midriff to calm the noise.

There was a ton of homework to do because I hadn't done any the night before. Half a chapter to read in earth science, twenty problems in math, sentences to dissect in English, pages to read in lit, two pages in the Spanish workbook. But I didn't feel like doing any of it. I was too scared.

What I wanted to do, what I *needed* to do, was talk to Suzanne.

First thing I did, though, I put a Band-Aid on my disgusting thumb. A SpongeBob Band-Aid. Can you believe it? They're the only Band-Aids we had in the house. Then I checked myself out in the bathroom mirror and redid my hair, quickly making a new ponytail, snapping the barrettes back in. I popped some gum in my mouth and, just for the heck of it, put on my fake Oakley sunglasses—my Foakleys—that Suzanne's older sister got for us cheap in New York City last fall when she went to look at a college.

On my way out, my grandmother was walking in with my mother. My grandmother lives in the town next to us, but it's only twenty minutes away so she stops by a lot. I didn't mind. I love my grandmother.

"Hi, Meemaw," I greeted her.

"Hello there, my darlin'," she said, cupping my face in her cold, bony hands. She kissed me on one cheek, then the other. And then she stepped back and started shaking her head. "Carlena!" she cried out to my mother, who was washing her hands off in the kitchen sink. "Look at this child! Look at how thin she is! You have *got* to make her eat."

Mom nodded sadly; she always does. But we're used to this kind of talk from Meemaw, and my mother does not have the energy to pursue it.

"Claire, sweetie, you're fading away," Meemaw moaned.

"I'm fine. I'm absolutely fine!" I assured her.

"And what's this I hear about your school? About some teacher?"

I glanced at Mom. We had decided last night not to tell Meemaw what had happened to me. She was too old, we figured, and the way she got upset, we didn't want to worry her.

My mother picked up a towel to dry her hands and shook her head. "The school's right on top of it, Mom. They won't let that guy back in to teach."

"Well, that's good," Meemaw agreed. She folded her hands over her enormous stomach and scowled. "They need to put that man in jail."

I didn't want to stick around anymore. "I'm goin' over Suzanne's," I announced.

When Mom took in a breath, like she was going to object, I added quickly, "Just for a minute, okay? Please. I *need* to see her, Mom. She wasn't in school."

My mother let her breath out. "All right," she agreed. "But be back before dinner."

I scooted out the door and took the sidewalk through my neighborhood to Suzanne's house, which was three streets away.

Of the three of us—Jenna, Suzanne, and me—Suzanne has the nicest house. It's in the part of our development that is newest and has, like, the biggest and most expensive homes with two-car garages, big front hallways, and spotlights in the front yards that come on at night and light up the bushes. Suzanne and her older sister each have their own rooms *and* bathrooms, and in the basement, there's a pool table and tons of exercise equipment. I was really jealous of Suzanne sometimes. At her house, every time you ate something, you could go down the basement and walk it off on the treadmill. At our house, even if we could afford it, we couldn't have any of that equipment on account of the kids.

When I rang the bell, I could hear the chimes inside. Suzanne came to the door right away and seemed glad to see me.

"You weren't in school," I said.

"No, my mom didn't want me to go." She looked over her

shoulder, then whispered to me, "She's lying down, resting. Do you want to walk over to the shopping center?"

"Sure." I nodded. "I don't have any money though."

"Hold on, I'll be right back." Suzanne disappeared into her house for a minute. She returned, pulling a denim jacket on and holding a five-dollar bill in one hand.

Softly, she closed the door to her house. We heard it latch. Then we fell in step and walked quickly down her front steps to another sidewalk on the street.

"What happened today?" Suzanne wanted to know.

I filled her in while we walked the two blocks to the play-ground, where there was a shortcut to the shopping center. I told her how everyone at school knew it was us who had told about Mr. Mattero. How Mr. Mattero wasn't allowed in the building, so we had a sub in music. How we got some sort of notice from Mrs. Fernandez at the end of the day. And how, at lunch, I found out Mr. Mattero had a daughter at our school.

Suzanne stopped and looked at me. "He *does*?"

"Yeah, in the eighth grade."

She groaned, but she didn't really say anything. What could you say?

We walked on.

At the playground, we saw a couple girls from our middle school sitting on the swings, talking, while they dragged their feet in the sand. They were sixth-graders, but we wanted to avoid them, so we hustled down the dirt path into a trashy ravine that took us over to the shopping center. It was a narrow path, with tall prickly bushes growing on either side so we had to go single file for a while and we didn't talk. When we came out near the Dumpster behind the Food Mart, Suzanne said, "Boy, we're really in it now, aren't we?"

Her expression matched my own. I knew we both felt bad and a little scared. "Yeah, we really are." I squashed a paper cup on the ground with my heel.

We walked on.

"My mother went to the Catholic school today and tried to enroll me," Suzanne said. "I begged her not to because I don't want to go there. We're not even Catholic! But my mom, she just wants me out of Oakdale. What am I going to do?"

"I don't know, Suzanne. But how can she send you there? I mean, will you have to wear one of those little kilts? You'll look like a geek, Suzanne."

"Thanks a lot, Claire! That makes me feel a whole lot better, you know?"

I was thinking of asking her if she would have to go to confession, too, only I could see Suzanne was depressed enough. And she was my friend—my oldest friend—after all. So I let up.

"Just tell your mom you want to stay at Oakdale. Ask her to give the school a second chance," I suggested. "Tell her it'll all blow over."

We walked on through the parking lot in silence. In front of the Dunkin' Donuts we stopped.

"Oh, my God," Suzanne said. She reached out and touched one of my silver earrings. "Where'd you get these?"

I grinned shyly 'cause I didn't want Suzanne to be jealous. "Jenna gave them to me."

Suzanne started smiling and put a hand over her mouth.

The grin fell off my face. "What? What is it?"

She brought her hand down. "I thought so. I was there when she got them."

"So?" I didn't know what she was getting at.

Suzanne widened her eyes. "Claire, Jenna *stole* those earrings from that kiosk thing at the mall. You know, the one with all the rhinestone barrettes and stuff."

"She did?"

"Yeah."

"Well, how was I supposed to know?"

Suzanne shrugged. I'm sure we were thinking the same thing, how Jenna had tried to get us to shoplift some makeup about a month ago, but Suzanne and I were way too scared. Plus it was wrong. We wouldn't do it. I kicked at a crack in the sidewalk. It felt a little embarrassing to be wearing something that somebody actually stole.

"Look," Suzanne said, "it wasn't *your* fault. You didn't steal them."

I looked up at her, and as I did I had a flashback to Jenna's room and all the nice stuff she always had, like that shirt from Abercrombie & Fitch, and the new purse. Gifts from her mother, she was always telling us. But come to think of it, her mother hadn't even been home the past few days! It gave me a stomachache thinking about this.

"Really. Forget it, Claire. Look, I'm getting a doughnut. You want one?"

I shook my head. "No. Just a Diet Pepsi, okay?"

Suzanne went into the shop and bought two sodas and a glazed doughnut, and we sat on the bus stop bench in front of the Hair Cuttery. It didn't even kill me to watch Suzanne eat that doughnut, I was so churned up inside. I examined the Band-Aid on my thumb. GO SPONGEBOB, it said. Patrick the Starfish was chasing a jellyfish, only you couldn't see the jellyfish because of the way the Band-Aid wrapped around.

"Cool," Suzanne said, noticing. "I love SpongeBob—especially his pet snail."

"Gary? Yeah, me, too," I said, smiling at her. "It kills me when he meows."

We started laughing, and lo and behold those kids from our middle school—the two girls on the swings—showed up across the way. I wondered if they had followed us from the playground.

We watched them come closer until they stopped in front us.

"Is it true?" one of them asked. "Are you guys the ones who reported on Mr. Mattero?"

We sat up. Suzanne shot me a frightened look. Instantly, her face got as red as her hair. I thought it was pretty bold of them to come right out and ask us that. It kind of made me mad, too. "Yeah, it's true!" I shot back. "Mr. Mattero did a bad thing."

For a second, I didn't know what they'd do. I braced myself for those girls to start blubbering about how we messed up the band competition. But instead, one of them said, "Wow. You must have been, like, really scared."

"Yeah, I wouldn't have known what to do!" the other agreed.

I think both Suzanne and I were surprised at their reaction. And seeing the sympathy we were getting, I guess that's what got Suzanne's courage up. I was so amazed because usually she's so shy and all.

"We weren't even doing anything," Suzanne told them, "just helping him put away play costumes, and he came in and put his arms around us."

"Yeah—we pulled away!" I exclaimed.

"I told him to stop!" Suzanne pointed out.

"But he felt us up anyway!" I added.

Both of those little sixth-graders sucked in their breath and looked like they were ready to pee their pants they were so shocked at what we said.

Suzanne and I turned to each other. I don't know if she was thinking the same thing as me, but I was, like, amazed at how much easier it was to talk about it now. Yeah. Like, *This is what Mr. Mattero did!* This is what happened to us on Monday after-noon in the band room at Oakdale Middle School.

14 Melody

I BUMPED INTO A CHAIR as I rushed from the cafeteria, then sprinted down the hall. My cheeks burned I was so horrified—and *so* embarrassed! In the girls' room, I took one look in the mirror and clapped a hand over my mouth. Some of the string beans dripping with tomato sauce were still plastered in my hair, and one of the slimy vegetables had slid down the side of my face.

Annie ran up beside me and gasped.

"It's okay, it's okay." I held up a hand and stopped her. "It's not blood; it's tomato sauce."

But Annie threw an arm around my shoulders anyway. She knew how much this had hurt. "Oh, my God, Mellie. They are so stupid—and *so* mean. I can't believe it! Those idiots!"

"Can you get me a paper towel?" I asked.

While she did, I plucked the mess out of my hair and threw the beans into the wastebasket. When Annie handed me the dampened paper towel, I used it to wipe off my face and hair.

Soon Jane, Noelle, and Liz stormed into the bathroom with the news that they had reported the incident to the teacher on lunch duty. Three boys, they said, had been taken to the office.

It was the longest day I ever spent in school. My hair was still sticky and matted from the gooey tomato sauce, and everyone could see it. I don't know how I got through two more classes and then homeroom, where we all received a special handout from the principal. I took one look and couldn't read it all because it was about Dad. I pushed the letter inside my Spanish book, which I shoved inside my backpack when the bell rang.

I had to be alone to read that note.

Annie waved to me over the crowd in the hall. "Call me tonight!"

I think I nodded to her, I'm not sure. I walked quickly to my bus. Sitting up front, I stared out the window while the others clambered on. *Hurry, hurry, hurry*, I said to myself, curling my toes inside my shoes and tapping the tips of my feet on the floor as I willed the bus to move faster.

Fortunately my bus stop was early. I was first off and walked fast. If my backpack didn't weigh a ton I would've run up the sidewalk.

I was glad when I didn't see any cars in the driveway or on the street in front of our house. At the side door, I fished the key out of my backpack, let myself in, then locked the door and went directly upstairs to my room. There, I dropped the heavy backpack on my bed and pulled out the Spanish book, which held the note. I smoothed it out on my lap and read it:

Dear Students, Parents, and Staff:

I want to inform you of a serious incident within our school that has had terrible consequences for several of our students and their families, as well as a member of our staff.

There will be a full investigation of this matter by the local police as well as by the school board. During that time—and afterward—I expect everyone in this school to respect the rights of each and every student here to attend classes and be a part of our school community without fear of verbal or physical harassment of any kind. Violators will be dealt with by me personally.

Thank you for your attention to this matter.

Mrs. Helena Fernandez, Principal

I read the note a second time, then a third, then folded and hid it beneath the jewelry box on my dresser. *A full investigation of this matter.* It made my father sound like a criminal!

Ashamed, uncertain—afraid of what it all meant, I wandered into the hall and sat on the stairs, pulling on my braid and thinking until Harmony rubbed up against me and nudged my arm to be petted. Beside me was a family picture, one of dozens that covered the wall the entire length of the stairs. I stared at the one closest, a picture of my father.

It was an old photograph, black and white, of Dad and his

jazz band a long time ago, before he was even married to my mother. In the picture, Dad has thick, brown wavy hair that touches his shoulders and a droopy handlebar mustache that makes him look like an outlaw. He holds a clarinet with his right hand, a cigarette in his left, and grins like a smart aleck. Dad says he was a crazy fool back then. He was an alcoholic, too. It was only after he met my mom at a friend's wedding that he became sober and started going to Alcoholics Anonymous meetings.

Mom is very proud of how my father recovered, and how he's stayed sober all these years, but my dad never says much about it and doesn't ever talk about those old days with the band. So the picture has given us—Cade and Song and me—countless hours of amusement and wonder. And sitting on the stairs that day, I really did wonder: was there something else secret about my dad's past? Was there something secret now? Why did those girls say those things about my dad? Was there *still* something we didn't know?

I stood up abruptly. I hated myself for even *thinking* that. How could I? Rushing back to my room, I changed clothes and got out of the house. The only place I could think of going was the horse barn. Stomping through the pasture, I hoped it wouldn't be a problem, me showing up even though it wasn't my day to volunteer. I didn't have my glasses on. I didn't wear them to the barns. But when I spotted someone in the paddock brushing a white horse, I assumed it was Mrs. Dandridge and lifted my hand to wave.

"Melody!" she exclaimed upon seeing me. She set the curry-comb down, wiped her hands on her jeans, and opened her arms to me. It was not a normal greeting; I guessed she had heard about what happened.

"You poor thing," she said. "I saw it on the news."

I let her hug me and squeezed my eyes shut.

After she pulled back, she held my arms. "Look," she said, "no one here knows—or cares, Melody. Certainly the kids don't!"

"Is it okay for me to come today? I'm not signed up," I said, trying hard not to cry and to keep my voice from trembling.

"Melody, you can come here whenever you want. There's always something you can do. Even if there's not, you can just hang out."

Shyly, I dropped my eyes, but I was grateful she understood. She was right about the kids. None of them even knew my last name.

"Calvin needs to come in," Mrs. Dandridge said gently. "Would you like to get him for me?"

I tried to smile, glad for something to do, and took a lead line to fetch the big bay from the pasture.

It was a beautiful spring day, cool, but with a high blue sky. Up until then I hadn't even noticed. When I returned to the barn with Calvin clomping beside me, some kittens skittered in front of us and chased each other the length of the barn. I felt better as I brushed the dirt off Calvin and picked a stubborn burr out of his long black mane. If only because I had something else to focus on for a little while.

By the time I returned home everyone else was back, too, including my father, who sat on his favorite recliner in the family room. The ugly bruise on his face had not gotten any better. Mom perched on the edge of the couch opposite Dad and nervously rubbed her hands together.

"What's happening?" I asked, stopping beside Cade, who leaned in the doorway with his shirt untucked and his thumbs hooked in his pockets.

Mom looked up at me. Her face seemed really tired.

"Your father couldn't take the lie-detector test today," she said. "The person who does them didn't come in. Maybe tomorrow, they said."

I felt really sorry for Dad. I knew he wanted to get it over with. "So that's no big deal, is it?"

Dad came to life. "Well, actually it might be," he said. "Your mother went online today and read up on it. She says polygraph testing has no scientific basis, that it's unreliable. Here," he said, picking up a printout from the coffee table in front of him. "Look at what that professor wrote. He said the test doesn't work. That it's always been prone to false positives."

I squeezed past my brother and went into the living room to take the papers from Dad's hands.

"What do you mean?" I asked. "Even if you're telling the truth, it can make you look like you're lying?"

"That's right," he confirmed.

I sat down on the couch beside Mom and heard her sigh. "Fred," she said to my father, "I told you yesterday I was worried about this."

Dad opened his hands. "But that detective—that guy, Daniels—he said they put a lot of stock in the lie-detector test. He said it would be pretty important for me to take it."

The four of us looked at one another.

"What about the lawyer?" Mom asked. "What did she say?"

I didn't even know they had talked to a lawyer.

Dad shook his head slowly. "She barely had time to talk to me."

"I don't like that woman!" Mom snapped. "She doesn't seem interested in your case, Fred. Maybe she doesn't believe you—"

"Mary!" Dad stopped her. "She's all I have right now, okay? She's the lawyer provided by the teachers' union. We can't afford to hire someone else. And she said I ought to take it."

Mom crossed her arms. "I don't know. I have a bad feeling about it."

Dad got up and walked over to the sliding-glass doors that opened onto our deck. He put his hands on his hips and stood looking out into the backyard for a long moment. "I don't think I have a choice," he finally said. "How's it going to look if I refuse?"

The next day, Mom picked me up after school so we could go together to get Dad at the police station. His car had a dead battery, and Mom had taken him to the station earlier for a one o'clock appointment. Cade was working, but Mom had the rest of the day off, and we had decided that after getting Dad, we'd take him out to eat, then rent movies, and drive over to Annie's house to pick her up.

It had been raining, and Mom pulled out an umbrella when we arrived at the police station. We huddled beneath it and picked our way around the puddles. It was at that moment that we ran into Jenna, who was leaving the station with her father. Only I didn't realize it was Jenna until we were inside, which is when it dawned on me how I knew Jenna in the first place— from the middle-school play!

"That's one of them!" I exclaimed, rushing to the window, where I could still see her walking to a car in the parking lot. Everyone knew the girls' names by now: Claire Montague, Suzanne Elmore, Jenna Cartwright.

Mom appeared beside me. "Which one?"

"Jenna Cartwright," I said. "She was one of the pirates."

"Pirates?"

"In *Peter Pan*," I explained impatiently. "The middle-school play."

There were over thirty pirates in the production, most of them sixth- and seventh-graders I didn't know, and all of them wearing eye patches and striped bandannas. But I recognized Jenna because of her long blonde hair with the red and brown highlights. Stupid highlights, I thought. I would never put a bunch of chemicals on *my* hair.

Even if she couldn't see me, I sneered at her. She never would have remembered me from the play because I was the crocodile, hiding out in my heavy papier-mâché head with many teeth and lying on my stomach on a skateboard, which is how I moved myself around.

I narrowed my eyes as the car Jenna was in drove away, and I felt angry, like I had missed an opportunity or something.

Just then, Dad came into the room quietly. He had his Redskins hat in his hand but no expression on his face.

Mom and I stood up, bracing ourselves. It was the kind of moment when you wished you didn't have to move forward, but you knew you had to.

"Well?" Mom asked carefully. "Did you pass?"

"Yes," he replied, without emotion. "I passed."

Mom and I rushed forward and threw our arms around him. We couldn't get Dad to share our enthusiasm, but it *was* a step forward. It was good news because we knew that lie-detector test was important to the police.

Finally, a small break, a little hope. We could breathe easier. We each put an arm around Dad and walked like that all the way down the sidewalk to the car. Then we celebrated by going to our favorite restaurant. Luigi's is just a little Italian café in a strip mall near our house. It's kind of tacky, with colored Christmas lights around the front windows and plastic flowers on the tables. But it has comfortable booths and soft lights— and Luigi's makes the best white pizza in the whole world.

It was still raining when we arrived. We made a run for it and stood inside the front door shaking the water off, and Dad actually smiled for the first time. We were seated right away, and in our corner booth, Mom handed out the menus. As I reached for mine, I noticed Mrs. Smith, an English teacher at my school, coming in with her husband, who is one of Cade's high-school football coaches. Mom saw them, too, and beckoned with her hand for the Smiths to come over.

Mrs. Smith waved back and held up a finger, like "wait a minute" because the waitress wanted to seat them.

"It's Lorraine Smith, and her husband, Jack," Mom leaned over to tell Dad, who was studying the menu. "I told them to come over."

"You're forgetting, Mary. They're not supposed to associate with me," Dad reminded her grimly.

"Oh, come on," Mom scoffed. "This isn't a courtroom. This is Luigi's!"

Dad's eyes didn't leave the menu.

"Should we tell them about the lie-detector test?" Mom asked.

My father barely moved his head. "It doesn't matter."

But a sparkle had returned to my mom's eyes. "Maybe I *will* tell them," she said, winking at me. "I think we ought to get the word out."

Dinner was great. Mom and I shared a white pizza, and Dad ordered his favorite ravioli Bolognese. We even talked a little bit about what we would do over the weekend, about planting some new azaleas and Dad grilling some of his short ribs. Mom kept glancing toward the front. I knew she was waiting for the Smiths to come over.

But the Smiths did not come over. As we paused by the front door, waiting for Dad to pay the bill, we peered into the other half of the restaurant and could see that the Smiths had already left—or, perhaps, had not stayed.

We rode quietly to the video store after that, the rain coming harder and smacking at the windshield. I offered to run in alone, and Mom pressed some money and the video-club card into my hand. Quickly, I picked out two movies, an old one Mom wanted, and a scary one for Annie and me. Then we swung by Annie's to pick her up for the sleepover at my house.

We were a little early, but I could see my friend, a dark silhouette, in the big picture window of her living room watching for me.

"I'll help her get her stuff," I said, taking the umbrella for the walk up to Annie's front steps.

When she opened the door, I greeted her and told her about the movie. "That scary one—the one we watched at Jane's, remember?"

"Come on in, Mellie," she urged. "Get out of the rain."

Inside the front door, I folded the umbrella carefully, trying not to drip all over their front hall. Annie wasn't smiling, and I worried that maybe she didn't like the movie I'd chosen. "Look we can always watch something else," I offered. "Cade's got a whole library of DVDs."

"It's not the movie," Annie said. "It's just that I can't . . ."

I waited. "Can't—what?"

"Go over to your house," Annie finished, dropping her eyes.

"Why not?"

Annie screwed up her face. "Look, Mellie. Maybe you could come over here instead."

At first, I was confused, but then a very cold feeling started to grip me. "What do you mean?"

Annie drew a breath. "My parents won't let me go."

My mouth dropped. I couldn't believe that because Annie and I were *best friends*!

"But you can come *here*, Mellie."

"Annie, you can't come over because of what those girls said?"

She pressed her lips together and met my eyes.

"You know my dad didn't do anything!"

She nodded and bit her lip. "I'm sorry."

I turned away from her, yanked open the front door, and left fast, not even closing the door behind me or putting the umbrella back up.

"Mellie?" Annie called after me. "Mellie! Please don't go away mad!"

But I didn't turn around. Not once while I walked down her sidewalk in the pouring rain. Not even after I slammed our car door shut.

(15) Claire

IT SOUNDED SO EASY. Sure. Put two fingers way, way back on your tongue to kind of gag yourself—and then heave-ho! But have you ever tried it? Huh? Because it does not work. Not for me anyway. All it did was get me worked up and frustrated. I don't know how those bulimia girls could do it. I'm telling you, if I could have, I would have, because every day I was coming home from school and eating way too much on account of I was so nervous. I hated myself for it, but I was really worried about getting fat again.

Fat and ugly. That's how I saw myself. "Disgusting," I even said out loud one night while I stared into the bathroom mirror. I had just brushed my yucky, thin, wispy hair straight back so I could wear a headband, but the headband made me look like a stupid clown. It's like I couldn't even do anything cool with my hair either.

I yanked the headband off and threw it in the sink. Then I

sat heavily on the lid to the toilet, checked out my poor, aching finger, and started crying.

A complete and total loser is what I felt like. It had been a week since we reported what Mr. Mattero did, and every day it seemed like things were getting worse, not better. Not that most kids said anything. Most of them didn't. Most kids at school didn't give a damn one way or the other! They were too busy with their own perfect little lives to worry about *our* problems. But there were some—those snotty little band members and the goody-goodies in the chorus—who gave us the evil eye every chance they got.

And every time I saw Melody Mattero I got a stomachache. She was easy to spot. No one else at school had a long braid like hers. Watching her walk through the hallway, her feet skimming the floor, her head hanging down, I knew she was hurting. Well, I was hurting, too, but no one knew it!

Suzanne and I were still friends. I was really glad she came back to school, that her parents gave Oakdale another chance. But she wasn't the same. She seemed incredibly quiet—even more than she was normally.

"Nothing bad will happen," I tried to tell Suzanne one afternoon at her house. We were in her basement, sitting on the floor beside all her exercise equipment shuffling cards, only neither one of us felt like playing anything.

"But I'm afraid," she said. "I mean, what if they believe Mr. Mattero and not us? Then what are we going to do?"

"I don't know." I kept shuffling those cards.

And that's when Suzanne's big sister, Addy, suddenly appeared like a bad dream from out of nowhere. She was home on a break from her college, and I guess she had been on the stairs eavesdropping, the little sneak. She came down with her arms crossed and her head cocked sideways, and she asked us straight out: "Did you guys lie?"

"What are you doing, spying on us?" Suzanne spit back at her.

Addy came closer. "Did you guys make up that stuff about your music teacher?"

Suzanne turned away. "Get lost," she muttered.

I kept my eyes on the cards and divided the deck into two piles.

But Addy stood right over us. "You better not have," she said. "You tell a lie like that, you'll have to *keep* lying to cover it up. And the more you lie, the more you'll have to lie."

Suzanne whirled around on her butt and tried to kick Addy right in the shins. "Bug off, freak!" she yelled. Let me tell you, a whole other side of sweet little Suzanne pops out when her sister's around. Not that Addy is always so evil. I mean, she did bring us those Foakleys from New York. But sometimes she's such a damned know-it-all. She was the first person in any of our families not to support us. I guess that's why Suzanne reacted so viciously. Plus we were both on edge.

Anyway, Addy wasn't the only person getting weird.

Jenna was acting a little strange herself. Like one day on the way to class she says out of the blue, "Claire, you're not selling me out, are you?"

"What are you talking about?" Honestly, I was completely baffled.

"Did you have that second interview with Detective Daniels?"

I stopped. We all three stopped. "Of course. Suzanne did, too," I said.

"We had to," Suzanne added.

"Did you tell him you couldn't remember some stuff?" Jenna asked.

"No! I told him everything I told him the first time."

Jenna zeroed in on me. "Then why did he tell me that? Why did he tell me you were having trouble remembering?"

"I don't know!" I fired back at her. "I didn't say anything different, and neither did Suzanne. Why would we? You think we *want* to get in trouble?"

Jenna backed off and held up a hand to stop us. "All right, all right. Forget it. Forget I said anything. I'm not mad."

We walked on, but then we paused at the water fountain. After Suzanne finished getting a drink, Jenna says to us, "Look, I've been thinking about something."

I rolled my eyes. I almost didn't want to know what it was, but Suzanne wiped her mouth and asked her, "What about?"

"You guys," Jenna said quietly, crooking her finger so we'd bend our heads close to hers. "I've been thinkin', like, how we need boyfriends."

"Boyfriends?" I repeated.

Suzanne giggled and shook her head like it was a joke.

But Jenna didn't laugh. "Seriously. They could protect us, you know?"

"Protect us from what?" I asked.

"Everything. All this crap that's going down."

I felt uncomfortable and looked away. I checked out my finger, which had a new Band-Aid on it—SpongeBob blowing bubbles. I didn't want a boyfriend! Well, not right then I didn't. I was glad when the bell rang. I walked off fast. So did Suzanne.

"I'm serious!" Jenna called after us.

But her words were lost in the crowd.

That *same* morning in earth science, when we had to pick partners for the weather project, Jenna slid her chair next to Danielle and Winston. I mean, what the heck? Jenna can't stand Danielle, and she wouldn't give the time of day to someone like Winston, who is sort of a nerd and, like, way too smart for *her*. So I don't know what Jenna was thinking, unless maybe she figured she could get a better mark working with those two geeks. The thing that really annoyed me is how she didn't even look at us.

See? We had just risked everything for our friendship with Jenna and she treated us like dirt. It annoyed me. Big time.

So Jenna was getting weird. But the real killer that week was the letter that came in the mail. It was addressed to my parents, Mr. and Mrs. Bradford Montague, in really nice handwriting. It wasn't signed though, so we never knew who sent it, only that it was an adult, someone with kids at school.

> Dear Mr. and Mrs. Montague,
> I feel compelled to write this letter out of sympathy for Fred Mattero, who has been nothing short of a fantastic music teacher to my three children at Oakdale Middle School—and a wonderful human being. For nine years I have watched him teach and have dealt with him in many capacities. I helped out in five different middle-school plays and accompanied Mr. Mattero on numerous field trips. Not once did I ever see him inappropriately touch a child, or ever make a lewd remark.
> You know what I think? I think three seventh-grade girls have either fabricated a story or blown something innocent way out of proportion. From what I understand, your daughter, and the two others involved, dress in extremely provocative clothing on a daily basis, as though asking for trouble. Tight jeans, bare midriffs, low-cut, clingy tops—this kind of attire has no place in middle school . . . blah, blah, blah.

That letter made me sick.

"It's that friend of yours! It's Jenna!" Mom exploded. "It's *her* influence!" Mom was really on the warpath, walking back and forth in the kitchen. It must've been like the twentieth time she read that stupid letter. "Jenna's been bad for you since day one!"

"It's not her fault!" I cried.

"But you didn't dress this way in sixth grade, at your other school!" Mom accused. "It's all since you started hanging out with that girl. I mean, look at the trouble you're in, Claire!"

"Well, since when do you care?" I hollered back at her. "All you do is worry about Corky! Your whole life revolves around him!"

That shut her up. Although instantly, I felt bad about what I blurted out. Sure, Mom worried about Corky. We *all* worried about Corky.

"What's going on?" Dad asked, coming into the kitchen after taking the kids upstairs to get into pajamas.

"It's that letter. I'm still upset," my mother complained.

"Well, don't take it out on Claire like that," my dad defended me. "She didn't do anything wrong!"

"But she's involved in this whole mess! And it's all because of Jenna. You know as well as I do Claire was never like this before. The clothes, the eye makeup, her grades! I mean, look at Claire's grades since she changed schools and met that girl!"

"That's not fair," I muttered. I felt bad about my grades going down. And so what if it was partly because of the time I spent with my friends? It was nice to have good friends like Suzanne and Jenna. And we didn't cause trouble. Well, what I mean is, we could do a lot of *worse* things! Like go to parties where they drink beer and smoke pot. We knew kids who did that stuff!

And if only my mom knew how Suzanne and I had put our feet down on the shoplifting, too. I flashed her a dirty look because I knew she could never understand. Not in a million years. I could not talk to my mother.

"Oh! And remember how Jenna wanted you and Suzanne to get your ear cartilage pierced? So you could be alike?"

True. It was true. We wanted to do that.

"You would have looked like a freak!" My mom was really losing it. "Next thing you know you'll want to pierce your tongue or something!"

"That's crazy," I argued. Jenna talked about that once, and I laughed at her because no way was someone punching a hole in my tongue. Although I did wonder if it would stop me from eating.

"You need to wake up, Claire!" Mom yelled at me.

Dad stepped in between us. "Carlena, take it easy," he said.

And just then Corky and Izzy came into the doorway, looking scared.

"Take a deep breath and calm down," Dad said to my mother, trying to put his arm around her.

But she shook him off and stormed out of the room. "You deal with it!" she shouted at Dad. A familiar phrase. We hear it a lot, only usually it's on account of a bad day with Corky, and believe me, there are a lot of bad days with Corky.

"Why Mommy's mad?" Izzy asked, her eyes wide and worried. Trailing her pink blankie, she started following my mother, but Dad scooped her up. "Come on, pumpkin," he said. "Let's go upstairs and look at a book."

It was a relief to have my mother out of the room. While Dad put Izzy back to bed, I took on my little brother. It was one of those weeks when Corky didn't want to sleep, so we snuggled up under the afghan on the couch. I must have read him ten different stories—plus did a little play thing with his whale puppet. He likes that. I pretend I'm a seagull friend of his whale. Finally, he let me take him up to bed.

When I saw Dad again, he was standing in the kitchen rereading that disgusting letter. "Those cowards—they didn't even have the guts to sign their names," he grumbled, tossing the paper on the table. "Who do they think they are?"

I agreed with Dad. Who *did* those people think they were? Because I am here to tell you that Jenna, Suzanne, and I did not dress different from most girls at school. Tight jeans, bare midriffs —that's the kind of clothes we *all* wore! Seriously, I was *not* dressing different. I mean, I would *kill* myself before I was different!

It was reaching a point. Every day, I thought, I just wanted to start over. I wanted to go to school and have friends and stick to my diet so I could lose more weight and maybe get a new dress and go to the spring dance. I just wanted all this stuff about Mr. Mattero to go away!

But it didn't.

The next week, Monday morning, I was hoping to make a

fresh start again when Sara Martindale, the eighth-grade class president, came on the intercom with morning announcements:

"Good morning, Oakdale Middle School. Today the sixth grade will have their eye exams in the health room during second and third class periods . . . Chess Club and Movie Club meet after school today . . . Lunch today is a cheese sandwich or a steak sub . . ."

I moaned silently, feeling for the box of Tic Tacs in my pocket.

"The quote for the day is from Bertrand Russell. 'To be without some of the things you want is an indispensable part of happiness.'"

I examined my torn thumbnail and wondered if I had to go without food in order to get skinny in order to be happy.

Next thing you know our principal's voice boomed over the intercom. "This is directed to members of the band and the chorus. The trip to Virginia for the competition has been canceled this year due to Mr. Mattero's absence."

A low groan went up in my homeroom.

I slid down in my seat.

"A partial refund may be possible," Mrs. Fernandez went on. "We are looking into it. That's it for now. Students, have a great day."

Have a great day, my foot. I knew there would be trouble now.

I just didn't know it could happen so quickly.

When the last bell rang, I went to my locker and discovered someone had busted the combination dial right off. Consequently, my locker door hung open, and you could see how, inside, all my things were gone—my books, my new pink windbreaker, my gym clothes I was taking home to get washed—even the little purple framed mirror that stuck on with magnets.

The only thing left in my locker was some trash and a bunch of nasty graffiti written with a permanent marker—the words "jerk" and "liar."

I looked around, but everyone was rushing for their buses.

Suzanne came up to me with tears in her eyes.

"You, too?" I asked her.

She nodded and wiped her eyes.

The same had been done to Jenna. But she didn't think we should tell anyone. "Don't show them we're weak," she tried to tell us.

"Who cares what they think?" I asked her.

"Yeah, who cares?" Suzanne echoed harshly.

"What am I going to tell my mother about my new jacket?" I asked Jenna.

"And how are we going to do our homework without our books?" Suzanne wailed.

Jenna grimaced.

We knew we had to report it.

In the office, we waited a long time to talk to Mrs. Fernandez. Each of us was allowed to use the telephone to call our parents. My mother and Suzanne's stormed in at the same time—I wondered if they came together—and went into the principal's office, closing the door behind them.

When they came out, they seemed only slightly calmer.

"This was the last straw," Suzanne's mother said as she took her daughter's hand. "I'm taking you out of this school."

My mother raised her eyebrows at me. "You, too, Claire. I asked for a transfer. You'll be going to a different school starting next Monday."

Astonished, I turned to Suzanne. We were both pretty shocked. But what could we do?

Mrs. Fernandez came up to Jenna. "Were you able to get hold of your parents?" she asked.

Jenna shook her head. "No. My dad's working construction, and sometimes he can't hear his cell phone."

"What about your mother?" Mrs. Fernandez asked.

Jenna hesitated.

"Jenna?"

"My mother doesn't live with us anymore," she said. "I don't know where she is."

Right away, it got her some sympathy from Mrs. Fernandez, who put an arm around Jenna's shoulders and took her into her office.

But I wasn't exactly weeping for Jenna just then. Not even if she did say her mother had left. Because really, like, who knew if that was true?

(16) Melody

NOT HAVING ANNIE FOR MY FRIEND WAS AWFUL. It left a huge, gaping hole in my life. But no way was I going to forgive her. My mother kept saying it wasn't Annie's fault, that her parents were to blame. But I think Annie could have stood up to them, and she didn't.

All weekend it kept going through my mind, over and over, how I had spun away from her. How I didn't even look back after I got in the car. My mother was horrified and my father absolutely outraged when I told them Annie couldn't come over to our house, but it was okay if I went to hers.

"Don't, Dad!" I had begged him as he angrily opened the car door.

Even Mom grabbed his arm to stop him, but he shook it off.

Together, we watched Dad stomp up the sidewalk through the pouring rain. He didn't take the umbrella or have a jacket on, so we knew he was getting soaked. Peering through the dark, trying to see, we'd held our breath while he rang the doorbell, then knocked loudly with his fist.

But no one ever returned to answer the door at Annie's house.

How could they do that to my dad?

When he returned to the car dripping wet, Dad simply started up the engine and drove away.

Didn't they know how humiliating that was?

The smell of Dad's wet wool sweater filled the car. He didn't say anything. He was so quiet it was scary. None of us spoke. And it hit me, riding home in that dark car, shivering and watching the back of my parents' heads, that my life was never going to be the same again. Not ever.

The next week, Mom went to work and Cade returned to school, but I refused. Dad didn't care, and Mom didn't argue. She said it would be okay for a few days and even went to school to gather books and deliver my homework. Most of my teachers were sympathetic. They sent back encouraging notes and long, detailed assignments so I wouldn't fall behind.

For a while, Dad kept himself busy with chores around the house. A couple times I tried talking to him while he worked: "Do you need some help? Do you want to go get an ice cream later?" But he was never interested. "I'm okay, Mellie. Just do your homework. I'll be fine." It was as though he had crawled inside himself. We all had, I guess. We had all crawled inside ourselves while we waited to see what would happen.

I think Mom was glad that I was home. "Call me if you get worried," she whispered urgently after pausing at the door on her way out one morning. She was fresh from her shower, her hair still a little damp, but her brows knit together with concern, and her eyes were red-rimmed from lack of sleep.

"What do you mean?" I asked, pulling on the end of my braid.

Mom pressed her lips together, thinking. "Just keep an eye on him," she said, "and call me if you think he's getting *too sad*."

We were all sad. Sad and angry and confused.

How would I know if my dad got *too sad*?

The schoolwork gave me something to do on the days home, but there was still a lot of time to fill. I didn't watch television because I knew how much it annoyed my father. Somehow he would know if the TV was on, even if he was outside, raking up leaves and sticks from winter and doing yard work. He must have filled fifteen black leaf bags for the garbagemen to pick up.

By about the third day we were home, there wasn't anything left to rake, so Dad started painting. He painted the downstairs bathroom. He painted an old set of bookshelves. He even repainted the chipped windowsill over the kitchen sink. I hoped he had another project lined up when the sill was done, because as long as he was busy, I didn't think he could get too sad.

One day I tried to cheer him up by fixing us a nice lunch. I set two places at the kitchen counter, where we have three stools. I even picked a daffodil from the front yard and settled it in a thin, silver vase between our two place mats. When the grilled cheese sandwiches were done, I put them on plates beside thick slices of dill pickle and a few potato chips.

"Dad!" I called cheerfully, leaning inside the door to the garage, where he was closing up paint cans. "I made lunch!"

My father seemed pleased. He looked up. "Thanks. I'll be right there."

After he came in and washed up, we sat down together. I noticed the bruise on his face was turning yellow and moving into a different stage, but I didn't say anything about it. Probably I shouldn't have said anything period. I certainly didn't mean to spoil it all by asking if he and Mom were going to rehearsal that night.

Dad looked startled. "Rehearsal?"

"Orchestra," I reminded him. Both my parents played in the community orchestra: Dad, second clarinet, and Mom, the flute. Wednesday nights, every week, they went to rehearsal. They were preparing for a Beethoven program in May.

Dad covered his eyes and moaned. "Oh, boy. And I wasn't

there last Wednesday either." Exactly one week ago the girls had accused Dad. Only seven days, yet in some ways it seemed like an eternity.

"Can you call Mrs. Branch for me, Melody? Tell her I can't make it tonight?"

I didn't want to call Mrs. Branch, the conductor. And I was disappointed in Dad for not going again, for just dropping out on them. I started to protest. "But it might be good—"

"I don't need a lecture," Dad cut me off. "I just need you to call Mrs. Branch for me."

He set his napkin down and pushed his stool back. "Thanks for the sandwich," he said in a gentler voice. Then he left, leaving the last bite.

Music had always been my father's passion—not just his job—and that gave me an idea. After reluctantly leaving a message for Mrs. Branch (I told her Dad wasn't feeling well) I dug out my viola.

"Dad," I said, after finding him on the back deck, where he was sanding the edges of the patio table, getting ready to spray paint. "Would you practice with me?"

My father played several instruments, and often, he would play the violin while I practiced my viola. He went back to sanding for a few seconds, then stopped.

"Just for twenty minutes?" I added quickly, during his pause. I thought surely some music would make him feel better.

He sanded some more, then straightened up and wiped the sweat off his forehead with the back of his hand. "Go ahead," he said. "Get started."

Feeling hopeful, I quickly retreated to the music room before he could change his mind. The music room in our house isn't very fancy. It's just a room next to the laundry that is half an office for my parents, who share a desk, and half a place to practice. But I like the room. A thick Oriental carpet covers the floor, and lots of green plants thrive in the two windows. One wall is taken up by an upright piano, while the opposite wall has built-in shelves full of music books, CDs, and old record albums.

Despite my mother's unending efforts, the music room is always a mess. I stepped carefully between the various instrument cases and pieces of music until I stood before one of the two metal music stands, rosined up the bow, and made sure the viola was in tune.

The music from when we last practiced just over a week ago was still up on the stand. I hadn't been very good that night. I was glad when Dad had finally said, "Enough." I remembered how we put away our instruments, and then how my father had opened his clarinet case. Whatever prompted it I don't recall, but I'd asked him why he had chosen the clarinet. Always having to put the instrument together, always having to change the reeds—he goes through dozens and dozens of them a year—it seemed like so much work.

"Love at first sound," he'd told me as he settled yet another new reed inside the mouthpiece. "I must have been five years old." Smoothly, expertly, he attached the mouthpiece to the barrel, the upper barrel to the lower barrel and then screwed on the bell. "It was when I first heard *Peter and the Wolf.* You know the part, where the clarinet is the cat, and there is that wonderful cadenza where the cat is trying to get the bird . . ."

Dad had lifted the instrument to his mouth, licked his lips, and played it for me. I smiled.

When he finished, he said, "See? I thought, what a great instrument. So much range and drama! Of course, I had to wait for my permanent teeth to come in, which wasn't for another three years."

I blinked, and the memory faded. I glanced at the clock. Fifteen minutes had passed since I asked Dad to practice with me. I turned toward the empty doorway and could hear him outside, sanding. He wasn't coming after all, I realized. I sighed and sat heavily in the chair at his desk, laying the viola across my lap. There was a new box of reeds in the pile on Dad's desk. An empty can of Diet Coke. A note to call the lawyer who represented the teachers' union. And a new, full bottle of sleeping pills. I didn't realize Dad was having a hard time sleeping, too.

There was no motivation to practice without him. Leaning over, I flipped open the viola case on the floor at my feet and settled the instrument inside. I would have been very sad to

know at that time what I know now. That the night Dad played
the cadenza from *Peter and the Wolf* was the last time I ever heard
him play his clarinet.

That same afternoon I was scheduled to volunteer at the barns
again, so I went upstairs to change. In my room, I scrutinized a
shelfful of horse statues. Each one was special and had been a
gift for either my birthday or Christmas. I cherished every one.
But really, what was I going to do with them all? I picked out a
gray horse that looked like Misty, the horse little Alexander was
supposed to ride, and set it on my bureau to take with me.

Downstairs, I found a small plastic bag for the horse and
dropped it inside. I had it with me and was walking out the
door when my brother burst through and brushed past me.

"Cade!" I exclaimed when I saw his eye, all red and swollen.
"What happened?"

He took the stairs two at a time with me right behind him.

"Were you in a fight?" I asked outside the closed bathroom
door.

The water was running. I heard him moan.

"Cade, do I need to get Dad? Answer me!"

Slowly, the door opened, and Cade looked at me while holding a wet facecloth over his eye. It was weird, the way it was in
almost the same place as where Dad was hit.

"I was in a fight," he mumbled. "But you don't need to tell
Dad."

"Is your eye okay?"

"Yeah, I think so."

"What happened?"

Cade pushed past me again, but I stayed right behind him, all the way down the hall to his room, where he sank down on the end of his bed.

"Cade, tell me, or I'll go get Dad."

"All right . . . all right." He gave in. "This kid, you don't know him, he picked a fight. Called Dad a bunch of names. I tried to ignore him, but he kept coming after me."

"Where were you? In school?"

"After school. In the parking lot."

When Cade took the facecloth off, I winced.

Cade actually grinned. "That kid? He looks worse than I do!"

"Oh, Cade . . ."

"Do me a favor, Mellie, will ya? Don't tell Dad."

"Don't you think he'll guess what happened?"

Cade pressed the cloth back against his eye. "I don't know. Probably. But he already feels bad enough."

It was getting to be a burden, feeling bad for Dad. I went downstairs to put some ice in a Ziploc bag and gave it to Cade. Then I closed the door like he asked and taped up a note: DON'T FEEL GOOD. TAKING A NAP.

It was tough, agreeing not to tell Dad. But I knew the truth would come out eventually. It always does.

———

The only good thing that day happened at the barns. Alexander actually came up to Misty and touched him on the nose. It was a quick little pat. But you could see how proud Alexander was of himself—and how surprised he was at the softness of Misty's nose. For a minute, I thought he might even let us help him into the saddle, but suddenly he turned and dashed back to his mother, where he clung to her legs.

I walked over and told him what a good job he'd done. "Maybe next time you can sit in Misty's saddle," I suggested, kneeling beside him. "In the meantime, Misty and I want you to have this."

Alexander peeked out at me from under one of the arms he had wrapped around his mother's legs.

I showed him the horse statue. "Here, you can take it home," I said.

With one small hand, he reached out and took hold of the horse. When I let it go, he pulled the horse away quickly and held it close to his chest.

"It's very kind of you, Melody. Thank you," his mother said.

But, as I said, it was the only good thing that happened that day.

When I got home, I took one look at Cade and Dad quietly standing in the kitchen with their arms crossed, and I knew that Cade had told him about the fight at school. He had to explain that eye somehow. Then, a few minutes later, Mom arrived, walking in with Detective Daniels, who told us the three girls at school were standing by their story.

"Not one of them has deviated or retracted a thing," Detective Daniels said.

Poor Dad. He was just so beaten down already.

"You're not going to file charges, are you?" Mom asked, a painful look consuming her face.

"I don't want to, Mrs. Mattero. Not with him passing the lie detector." He looked at Dad. "We'll give it a little more time, Fred, but if they stand by their story, I want you all to know I might not have a choice."

(17) Claire

AT ALPHONSO P. DECKER MIDDLE SCHOOL I made a fresh start. Let me tell you, it was a relief to put the past behind me.

Nobody knew me at Decker. They didn't have a clue that I was one of those three seventh-graders at Oakdale who had accused their music teacher of sexual abuse. As far as they were concerned I was just a regular girl. At least I hoped that's how they saw me. A regular girl, but kind of shy, maybe—and *thin*. Thin with brown hair and a new fake leather jacket and a sense of humor. I mean, you had to have a sense of humor to wear double SpongeBob Band-Aids, right? (But I was worried I had an infection on my finger by then and didn't want Mom to know.)

Anyway, Decker is like twenty-five minutes from my house, so every morning I went with Dad when he left for work. It was sort of nice starting out the day with my father. He works for a company that makes medical-technology software (how boring is that?), so there's not much we can talk about there.

Instead, we talked about me, about the classes I took and the kids I'd met. We even hit on what I wanted to do that summer, and I surprised myself by blabbing away about how we ought to go on a family trip somewhere. "Instead of just the beach, which we always do, why don't we, like, go see something? Maybe the Grand Canyon? Or that place in Florida where you swim with the dolphins?" Man, I have always wanted to do that. Dad seemed interested. He actually said he'd talk to Mom.

At Decker, I was pretty quiet. But I tried harder. I took notes and listened in class. I still wore the same kind of clothes, but my mother put her foot down on makeup. "Be more outgoing," she preached, "instead of depending on all that eye goop to make an impression."

Not that I totally listened. I mean, I did sneak a little eyeliner to school in my pocket. But I also tried to smile more at kids.

I don't know. Maybe it kind of worked because my second day at Decker, this girl came up behind me while I stood petrified by that huge cafeteria full of strange faces. "Hi, Claire," she said. When I swung around, there was this really cute girl with long brown hair and a fantastic smile.

"Hey," I replied warily, wondering how she knew my name. I mean, she didn't look psychic or anything.

She lifted her eyebrows. "I'm in your English class."

"You are?"

She chuckled. "Math, too."

"Gosh, I'm sorry, I didn't recognize you. So many kids and all—"

"It's okay. Don't apologize." When she blinked, it looked like she had on cucumber eye shadow.

"I was new earlier this year," she said. "I know the feeling."

"You do?"

"Yeah."

I'm not sure, but I think she had on lavender mascara—that and the green eye shadow made a nice combination.

"Look, do you want to sit with me?" she asked. "For lunch?"

I squeezed my shoulders together and lifted them. "Sure," I said.

The girl's name was Phoebe. And she changed everything.

I never knew anyone named Phoebe before. It was a funny name, I thought. It sounded funky and old-fashioned, but kind of cute, too.

At first, I wondered why she was paying so much attention to me. It was a little like when Jenna first came to Oakdale and cozied up to Suzanne and me, and I wasn't so sure now of how good a friend Jenna had turned out to be.

But as the next couple weeks went by I stopped being so suspicious because—this is really incredible—Phoebe and I had so much in common! Like we were the oldest of three kids in our families, we were born in August, and our favorite movie of all time was *Lord of the Rings*. Plus, we both had younger brothers with special needs. I told her all about Corky and his allergies and how my mom thought that made his autism worse. And she told me all about Greggie, her little brother with attention deficit.

"We ought to get them together," I said.

"Can you imagine?" Phoebe replied. "It would be a disaster!"

I laughed, only I don't know why because it wasn't funny, not really. Poor Corky, he didn't have any friends at his kinder-garten—not a single one—because normal kids didn't have the patience for him. They didn't know how smart he really was, or why he stood there watching them while he rocked side to side on his feet, or why he didn't say anything when they asked him what his name was because some weeks he just plain didn't talk.

That first day Phoebe and I ate lunch together, we sat down and while I took the apple out of my backpack, Phoebe zipped open an L.L. Bean lunchbox that had an enormous pile of food in it: a turkey and cheese sandwich on whole-wheat bread and little zip baggies full of carrots, orange sections, potato chips, and cookies. She even had a yogurt—the custard kind—and a carton of chocolate milk! I am not kidding, Phoebe ate more at lunch than I ate in an entire day. And she wasn't fat at all. Not a lick!

When she saw me staring at her food, she blushed. "I get so hungry," she explained. "But after school I swim, and I would never make it if I didn't have the energy."

"You swim? What, is there a swimming pool or something in this school?"

"No. But the swim center isn't far away," Phoebe said. "We take a bus. It's more like a club than a team, really. You should join." She bit into that enormous sandwich. "Do you swim, Claire?" she asked around a mouthful.

"Oh. Yeah. Sure, I swim, and I like to and all that, but I've never been, like, on a team before." Meanwhile, my mind was spinning and doing all these incredible calculations. I knew that swimming for one hour burned four hundred calories—so two hours would be twice that, right? And eight hundred calories was awesome! It was no wonder Phoebe could eat a big lunch.

"You should come. You should try it," Phoebe encouraged me.

Imagine, I thought, eating all that food *and* staying skinny. "I will," I promised her. "I'll talk to my mom."

Over lunch (I stuck with my apple, but I accepted half of a half of one cookie) Phoebe told me all about herself. How her parents got divorced and then how her mother had just been remarried to a guy she didn't like and how, because of his job, they had moved here from Kentucky.

I knew she expected me to tell her my story, too, so I had to think fast. I couldn't tell her what really happened because she wouldn't want anything to do with me. Instead, I told her I had lived in North Carolina. I knew a little about North Carolina because of my cousins who lived down there.

Phoebe seemed surprised, but then she said, "Cool. We went to the beach once in North Carolina."

I took another mouse nibble on my cookie. "We lived more inland," I said. "This town called Greensboro."

Phoebe kept eating. Waiting for me to say more, I guessed.

"You probably wonder why we had to move up here." I watched Phoebe open her yogurt. "My dad's job," I said. "He got hired by a software company in Washington, D.C." I knew she wouldn't ask questions about that 'cause nobody understands what my dad does.

"It's sad, leaving your old school, isn't it?" Phoebe sympathized.

I shrugged like no big deal. "Not really. There were a lot of hicks down there. And now we have a new house so that's kind of fun." I started to describe the house that Suzanne lived in, but then I thought, yikes, what if Phoebe came to my house one day? Then she'd know I didn't have my own bathroom and all that exercise stuff in the basement. So I kept to the facts on that one. Before returning to class, we traded telephone numbers and e-mail addresses and that night, after Phoebe got home from swimming and had dinner, we checked our math homework online.

We ate lunch together the rest of the week, and I wove together quite a story for Phoebe about who I was. Too bad there wasn't a creative writing class in the seventh-grade at Decker. I bet I could've aced it.

———

At home, I was turning over a whole new leaf, too. I did my homework before I turned on the television. And I took care of Corky and Izzy every afternoon so Mom could take a walk. Plus I let her teach me how to make Noah bread, which is the only kind of bread Corky can eat because there's no wheat in it. We also made some ice cream for Corky one night—ice cream with potato milk! It wasn't bad either.

I really missed Suzanne, who'd gone to the Catholic school. I wondered if she had to pray a lot and go to religion classes. But I wasn't allowed to talk with her or with Jenna.

I tried not to think about Mr. Mattero or his daughter Melody. I guess I figured that things would just go away once I had left Oakdale Middle School. That people would forget about it—and just get on with their lives.

So, like I said, that first week at Decker I was feeling pretty good about things. The second week I felt even better. I paid attention in class and was really nice to everyone, especially Phoebe. We even hooked up one day at the mall and went to the pet store to play with the puppies, and I hadn't done that in ages (Jenna always thought it was too babyish). Hey! And get this—we had lunch in the food court: chicken nuggets dunked in honey, waffle fries, coleslaw—a *roll*. We even had a chocolate-chip ice-cream cone at Maggie Moos for dessert.

It was soooooo incredibly good, and even if we had walked around the mall enough to burn up about a thousand calories,

I still felt guilty. "I can't believe I ate all that," I moaned, chucking the end of my cone into the trash.

Phoebe elbowed me. "But Claire, you're so skinny! And you know, if you went swimming with me, you could eat what you wanted every day!"

She wasn't giving up on me—she really wanted me to join that swim club of hers. I was seriously thinking I'd try it.

Almost three weeks had gone by, and Phoebe and I were getting to be really good friends. She slept over my house three different times—she actually asked me two of those times if she could—and we had so much fun. We watched all three *Lord of the Rings* movies. We painted our nails. And we did silly things I hadn't done in years, like Spirograph with colored pens and Twister, which was nuts. One night, we even hauled out my old Barbies from a box under my bed and dressed them up, just for fun. Another time, Phoebe asked me to trim the ends of her hair, so you know she must have trusted me like a whole lot.

Everything was kind of moving forward.

Then along came Jenna to spoil it all.

18 Melody

JENNA CARTWRIGHT. Claire Montague. Suzanne Elmore. I knew their names by heart now. And I hated those girls. *Hated* them.

I dreaded going back to school. But after missing so many days, I had to return. Mrs. Fernandez had sent home a note offering to give me a transfer to another school if I was too uncomfortable. But Oakdale Middle School was *my* school. It was where my dad taught. It's where my friends were! I couldn't just give it up.

At least one thing made my return easier: the news that two of the three girls had gone to different schools. Suzanne to a Catholic school and that girl, Claire, to another public middle school somewhere in the county.

Still, Jenna was at Oakdale. And Annie was there, too, constantly trying to get my eye and hanging out by my locker. Maybe I shouldn't say "constantly" because after I completely ignored her a few times, she gave up. Most of my other friends welcomed me back. Jane gave me a hug. Liz and Noelle saved me a place at lunch. And no one said anything—or threw food.

But as time went by, it became more awkward, instead of easier, to be at school because Annie and I had the same friends. Some days, I didn't even go to lunch, but just walked the halls, or sat in the library and thumbed through a magazine. I stopped going to the lit magazine meetings, and the one time I took out my notebook to work on a poem, all I did was stare at the empty page. I even faked being sick so I could stay home on Crazy Hair Day. I was not in the mood for it.

The bruise on Cade's face faded, like Dad's. But the pain of how and why it got there in the first place never went away, not for any of us. It's just that we all dealt with it differently. My brother simply shut himself off. Whenever he was home, he stayed in his room with the door closed and his music on. He was even allowed to take his dinner up there.

My mother worked. Fourteen hours a day and weekends, too. Spring was the nursery's busy time, with so many people planting and getting their gardens ready. Every day, Mom came home exhausted, with dirt under her fingernails and the smell of mulch clinging to her clothes. She made dinner and then— here's the really strange thing—every evening she went out in the backyard and pulled weeds as though she were obsessed.

We had a huge backyard, all of it bordered with ivy, and in the past year a vine called Virginia creeper had invaded and practically taken over. The task of pulling all the weeds out by hand seemed overwhelming, especially since the creeper twisted itself around the ivy vine. You had to practically sit down and untwist the bad vine from the good vine before you could pull it out. Even Cade couldn't believe what Mom was attempting. "It's like taking truckloads of water out of the ocean," he observed one night, shaking his head as we watched our mother. "Why bother?"

"Maybe she just needs something to do," I replied. It was good that Mom had something to keep her occupied because there wasn't anything we could act on to make our situation better. We were stuck! We were just waiting.

The waiting was hardest on Dad. Almost a whole month had gone by, and he seemed more and more lost. He had run out of chores, too. Either that, or part of him just gave up. He slept late and puttered around the house. He never touched his clarinet. Both he and Mom dropped out of community orchestra. Eventually, I stopped practicing, too, because there was no one at school to direct the band or the orchestra.

Even though he was home all day, Dad didn't lift a finger to help with supper. One day, he even forgot to take the hamburgers out to thaw, and it was the only thing Mom had asked him to do. I thought it was a real comedown for him when he started watching television—at first, old movies and episodes of *Stargate,* and later, anything that was on. And then, he started taking afternoon naps. One time he locked himself in his bedroom and fell so deep asleep he didn't hear me knock.

One of the only things I looked forward to during that time were e-mails from my sister at college, which never failed to make me laugh. Her e-mails, and my cat.

My job at the barn kept me going, too. My own problems seemed like a drop in the bucket compared to most of the kids who came for riding therapy. Some of them couldn't tie their own shoes, or put one foot in front of the other. There was one little boy who couldn't even sit up on the horse. Mr. Hibbard, one of the volunteers, had to grab him by the back of his shirt to keep him upright while he went around the ring on Daisy Mae. The great thing about the riding, though, is that it gave those kids such a boost. It was fun for them, and I don't think there was much fun in their lives. Plus, it must have given them such a sense of accomplishment riding around the ring on a big horse.

Even Alexander finally got his courage up and sat on Misty for the first time. He was so pleased with himself he practically burst. Quietly, so as not to scare the horse, we all cheered and patted our hands together. We made him promise to try riding around the ring next time. "You stay," he said, pointing a finger at me. It was the first time I'd ever heard him say a word.

"I'll be right here beside you," I assured him. On days like that, when I walked home from the barn, it was hard to feel sorry for myself.

My sister called home from Indiana during this time to tell us her exams were over, and not one of us let on what had happened to Dad. We didn't want to drag her down, too. She was excited because a friend at college had invited her to go to Chicago to see a play.

Then Detective Daniels stopped by one night.

"I've interviewed all three of those girls again," he said. "They stand by their story, one hundred percent."

My mother sucked in her breath.

Dad didn't say anything.

We understood that his visit was a warning: to get ready for what was going to happen next. We all knew *something* had to happen. Still, I wasn't prepared for what happened next, for the day I came home from school and couldn't find my father.

Dad's car was in the yard, but he didn't answer when I called. He wasn't in the backyard. He wasn't in the garage. The television was off. Right away I had a bad feeling about it.

I started checking each room, the laundry, the music room, and when I entered the bathroom, I stopped. On the counter by the sink were two empty sleeping pill bottles.

"Dad?" I called out as I scooped up the empty bottles.

My heart started pounding.

"Dad! Answer me!"

I felt like I was in a horror movie as I ran from one room to the next, searching, and all the time dreading what I might find. I kept telling myself that my father wouldn't hurt himself. He wouldn't do something like that because of what those stupid girls did.

Would he? Would he do that?

"Daddy, where are you?" I hollered, rushing down the hall.

(19) Claire

"I'M NOT SUPPOSED TO talk to you, Jenna," I warned. I didn't even open the door all the way. "And I'm not allowed to have anyone over when I'm babysitting."

Jenna stuck her head in anyway and widened her eyes. "Like I'm really dangerous?"

I glanced at the clock and saw that my parents weren't expected home from their party for another three hours.

"Claire, come *on*!"

I sighed and stepped back. "All right. But just for a little while, okay?"

Jenna squeezed herself in. "You are such a dweeb sometimes, you know it?"

Softly, I pushed the door closed and locked it.

When I turned around, Corky and Izzy ran up to us.

"Hey there!" Jenna greeted them. I have to admit she's really great with little kids, and both Corky and Izzy loved her. Izzy was in her fairy princess outfit and waved her wand at us. "I turning you to frogs," she kept saying until we both had to crack up.

But Corky wasn't talking. He stood behind me quietly until Jenna bent down and said, "Hey there, Cork!" Beaming, he held up a big rubber elephant for her to see. "Wow!" Jenna responded. "Where's the baby?"

We had a whole bin full of jungle animals, whole families of different kinds. Corky ran off to find the baby elephant, and Izzy trailed behind him.

Jenna straightened up and put her hands in her back pockets. She was wearing a pretty new V-neck top with colored stripes, and crisp new white capris. Her hair was in a ponytail, and she wore three sets of sparkly green rhinestone earrings that matched her eyes and some of the green stripes in the shirt. I felt pretty dumpy beside her in my cargo pants and a baggy sweatshirt that had a hot chocolate stain on it.

"Those kids are so cute," Jenna said. "Is Corky still collecting corks? And how's he doing anyway?"

"No, he doesn't collect corks anymore. He's onto rocks. And actually he's doing pretty good. He's been on a special diet 'cause of his allergies, and we think it's helping. He doesn't get so ornery. Or do things over and over, the way he used to."

Jenna knew what I was talking about. One night when she was at our house, my brother sat on the kitchen floor opening and closing the cabinet door under the sink for, like, an hour.

We followed the kids down the hall toward the family room,

where Izzy was curled up on the sofa in her sparkly dress, sucking her thumb and already engrossed in an Elmo video.

"How's your new school?" Jenna asked.

"All right, I guess." I wrinkled my nose. I didn't want her to know how much I liked the new school and how I was going to swim club the next week. I even had a new navy blue tank suit for it. It was in a bag in my room, with new goggles and silicone ear plugs.

Jenna leaned over and whispered, "Can we go up to your room for a minute?"

"I guess so," I said. But when we got there, I didn't want her to see my new swimming stuff, so I grabbed the plastic bag off my bed and threw it in the closet, like I was making places for us to sit. Then I sat cross-legged on my bed.

Jenna pulled out the chair at my desk. "What's this?" she asked, picking up an index card. She read out loud what I'd written: "Violence is any mean word, look, or act that hurts a person's body, feelings, or things."

"Just a saying," I told her. I picked up my stuffed platypus and hugged him. "It's on the bulletin board in my new social studies class."

"How come you wrote it down?"

I shrugged. I couldn't tell her how deeply I had thought about those words. Like I didn't realize that just saying something could be considered an act of violence.

Jenna put the card to one side. "So, have you heard?" She

had this sly little grin on her face. "Matt Lewis and I are going out."

"You *are*?" I tried to sound nonchalant, but inside I was thinking, *What a creep! Matt Lewis with his spiky hair and his Goth clothes?*

Jenna stroked her ponytail, which had fallen over her shoulder. "Yeah, he's really, really nice."

So Suzanne and I had already been replaced by Matt Lewis. A *boyfriend*. Was that what she came over to tell me? To rub it in my face that she had a boyfriend now?

"We won't be together long though," Jenna continued, examining her fingernails, like she was already bored being at my house. "'Cause we're moving, my dad and I, to Pennsylvania, near my grandmother in Lancaster."

I leaned back againt my pillows and stared at her.

Jenna paused. And then the shocker: "I just want you to know I'm sorry, Claire. I never thought it would go this far."

She didn't have to explain any more. I knew she was referring to the enormous lie we had told about Mr. Mattero. "Me neither," I said quietly.

"We can't say *anything* now. Right?"

"*Right*." I nodded, agreeing with her. We had to keep our mouths doubly shut because it would be so incredibly embarrassing now.

"I mean, can you imagine if we told everyone what happened? Mr. Mattero would probably choke my dad to death on the spot!" Jenna laughed, but it was a nervous laugh. "Either that, or he might grab one of *us* or something. God, it would be wild. It would be *awful!*"

I shook my head, and I wasn't laughing. "We would never have to say anything in front of Mr. Mattero. He would never even be in the same room as us unless we were in court or something. That's what Detective Daniels said."

"He told you that?"

"A couple times."

Jenna sat up and scowled. "What? Did you ask him about it, Claire?"

"Chill!" I said, staring right at her. "I didn't *ask* him anything. It's what he told me. He said no kid would ever have to come forward and tell the truth with a bunch of other people in the room—especially not Mr. Mattero. He said it would be too whatchamacallit—intimidating."

Jenna sank back in the chair at my desk and fiddled with a paper clip. Neither one of us said anything. One by one, I folded the felt feet of my platypus under his belly.

"Whatever," Jenna finally said. "I just feel sorry we did it because now we're all split up. Plus, you know, one of the main reasons I did it was to get my mom to come back, and it didn't work."

I put my platypus down. "What do you mean?"

She smiled sarcastically. "Can you believe it? I actually thought my mom would feel so bad about it that she would come home. But look what happened—it *backfired*. She didn't come back, she left!"

I frowned at her. "I thought it was to get out of Mr. Mattero's boring music class. And to get back at him—for you not getting the Wendy part in *Peter Pan*."

Jenna sighed. "It was . . . a little bit, I guess." She put the paper clip down. "But it's a good thing I didn't get that part. I'm not a very good singer."

"Jenna!" I did not find that funny, although really, it didn't much matter what Jenna's reason was. Suzanne and I went along with her because we were friends and because Jenna asked us to—and yeah, the truth is maybe I wanted a little attention from *my* mother, too. But that's not why I did it. The absolute main reason was the friend thing. We never once thought it would create all these problems or that anyone would get hurt.

"The whole thing was pretty stupid," I said. I plucked at a loose thread in my bedspread. "We never should have said those things about Mr. Mattero."

"Oh, Claire!" Jenna sounded disgusted with me. "Who cares what happens to Mattero? He's such a creep. Honestly, sometimes I don't know why I wasted my time on you."

"Excuse me. *Wasted your time?*" I asked, a little stunned at that statement. "Is that—"

"You know what?" She threw up her hands. "I don't care

about anything anymore. Why should I? My mom doesn't care about me! For a whole year, she was seeing that guy when she told us she was flying. I mean, *what a liar!* All those times she went to Hawaii and brought us those nuts?"

"The macadamias?"

"Yeah! She bought them at the grocery store!"

My mouth fell open a little.

"I hate her so much! She never cared about me. She never even bought me half that stuff I was always showing you guys."

Pause. "She didn't?"

"No."

"Then where'd all that stuff come from?" I asked, although I don't know why I bothered because I think I knew the answer.

Jenna slumped back in my chair and turned to stare at the wall. Her shoulders moved a little, like she was crying. I don't know, I was mad at Jenna, but I felt sorry for her, too. I think she was really messed up by her mother.

I got up off the bed to get her a Kleenex just as Corky ran into my room. He held a gray horse out to Jenna, and she recovered so quickly I wondered if she really had been crying.

"Hey there, buddy," she laughed, then sniffed, "that's not an elephant baby!"

I think we were both glad to be distracted.

Corky snatched the horse back and ran from the room.

"He carries that thing around with him all the time now," I told her.

"Why?" Jenna wiped her cheeks, and I could see they were wet. "Is he into cowboys or something?"

"No, some girl at this place where Corky takes riding therapy gave it to him." I lowered my voice in case Corky was outside the door. "It looks just like the horse they want him to ride, only he's too scared."

"Ahhhh . . ."

Pretty soon after that, Jenna got up and left. I was glad.

A week or so later, I heard she was gone. Moved to Pennsylvania with her dad, just like she said.

But I still don't think it's fair. How she missed all the fallout.

(20) Melody

"CADE!" I SHOUTED, running to meet my brother as he drove up after school. "I can't find Dad!"

My brother does not panic easily. He frowned at me through the open window and didn't even soften the radio in his car. "So? Maybe he's takin' a walk or something."

"Dad doesn't take walks. And look—" I held out the empty bottles of sleeping tablets.

Cade raised his eyebrows and turned down the music. "What's that?"

"I found them by the bathroom sink."

The expression melted from Cade's face. He turned off the ignition. "What? You think he overdosed or something?"

"I don't know," I answered. At the same time, it hit me that I hadn't checked upstairs in the house. "Maybe he's taking a nap," I suggested, hoping that's all it was—a nap—even though it didn't explain the empty bottles.

"Mellie, wait!" Cade called as I ran back toward the house.

But I was not waiting for my brother.

Inside, I flew up the stairs and raced down the hall to where his bedroom door was closed.

"Dad!" I called, rattling the knob on the locked door. "Dad! Are you okay?"

No answer.

Cade rushed up behind me.

I pounded on the door. "Daddy! Are you in there?"

When he didn't answer, my brother and I looked at each other.

"Cade, I'm so afraid of what Daddy's done!"

Cade shook the door, too, but nothing happened. "Dad!" he called out, even louder than I had.

When there was no response, Cade ordered me to "stand back." Then he turned sideways, lifted his right shoulder, and threw his weight against the door. Nothing. He tried again but the door didn't budge.

Next, Cade took a step backward, lifted his foot, and kicked the doorknob. His heel smashed the knob off, and it clattered to the floor. Slowly, the door squeaked open.

When we rushed in, we saw my father sprawled facedown on his bed.

"Daddy!" I screamed.

Cade ran over and shook his shoulder.

I held my breath.

"Dad, are you okay? Are you okay?" Cade kept asking.

I brought my hands down. "Should I call for help?"

When Cade didn't answer, I rushed to the other side of my parents' bed, but their cell phone wasn't where it usually was on the nightstand. In a panic I swung my head around, searching. "I can't find the phone!"

"Dad!" Cade called.

I spotted the phone on the floor and picked it up.

But Cade yelled, "Wait, Mel!"

I looked up to see him holding up an empty vodka bottle.

And Dad moaned.

"He's drunk," Cade said. "Drunk as a skunk."

"Daddy's *drunk*?" I uttered in disbelief. I brought the phone down. I had never seen my father take a drink, let alone be drunk.

"Hey? Whas goin' on?" Dad asked sleepily. He tried to push himself up on his elbows and open his eyes, but they kept closing. He looked at Cade, then slowly turned his head toward me. What little hair he had was rumpled, and he wore a dumb, rubbery expression on his face.

"Dad, we thought you overdosed or something," Cade said. "Mellie was just about to call 911."

Dad pushed himself to a sitting position beside Cade.

"D–don' do that," he said.

"But what about these empty bottles?" My voice shook. I thrust the two empty containers toward him. "I found these in the bathroom downstairs."

My father hung his head. "Yeah." He took in a breath and blew the air out. "I dumped 'em out. I dumped 'em in the toilet."

"What?" Cade seemed perplexed.

But I caught on right away. "So you wouldn't take them, Dad?"

He covered his eyes and didn't answer.

I left the room—I had to get out—and went downstairs to make coffee. In all the movies I had ever seen, drunk people sobered up with coffee. While it dripped, I paced the kitchen, still in shock over what my father had done—and *almost* done. Then, when the coffee was ready, I poured it into a mug, added milk and sugar, and took it upstairs, walking carefully so as not to spill it.

"Don't bother," Cade said, meeting me in the hallway. "He's dead to the world."

I flashed him a startled look.

"As in dreamland," Cade clarified, arching his eyebrows. "Just let him sleep it off, Mel."

Still, it was a poor choice of words, I thought.

We went downstairs together.

"Should we call Mom?" I asked, setting the steaming mug down in the sink.

Cade wrinkled his nose. "Nah. I wouldn't. What's she going to do? It'll just upset her."

So we didn't call Mom. We waited until she came home from work to tell her. She placed a bag of groceries and a gallon of milk on the counter and, without even putting any of it away, sat down on a kitchen chair.

"I was afraid of this," she said.

"Afraid of what?" Cade asked.

Mom's weary eyes settled on him. "I was afraid he'd relapse and drink because he's depressed. Because of the pressure he's been under."

"It could have been worse," I offered.

Mom nodded wearily. "Yes. It could have been worse. I wonder if I need to get him some kind of help. And gosh, it's going to be so embarrassing for him. On top of everything else that's happened, he'll have to deal with this."

Mom added, "I just hope you kids don't think any less of your father because of what he did today."

Would I? Would I think less of Dad?

I wondered about that all evening.

Even after Dad had sobered up and come downstairs to apologize to us, I wondered whether I thought less of Dad.

"There's no excuse for what I did. No excuse at all," he said. "I am so sorry, Cade. Mellie. Please forgive me."

Even after he said that and didn't touch a bite of dinner and sat in the family room all evening, just sat in his chair, without the television on, or a book or anything, I still wondered about it. Because as hard as I tried, I could not get that image of my father with his dumb, rubbery expression out of my head. It's like all of a sudden, he wasn't even the same person I knew anymore.

A couple more days passed, and still we waited for word from Detective Daniels. As I said earlier, one of the only bright spots during that time was my job at the stables. But it was yet another bubble that burst the following week.

I arrived early on my volunteer afternoon to brush and tack up Misty. I even gave the horse a pep talk and told him to step very carefully when he took Alexander around the ring for the first time. I looked forward to being one of the two walkers who would accompany Alexander on his first trip. Another volunteer would lead the horse. When the boy arrived, however, he came with his family.

"Melody," Mrs. Dandridge said, accompanying the family and eager to introduce me to the girls. This is Isabelle, Alexander's little sister."

I shook hands and smiled at the small, blonde-haired girl.

"And this," Mrs. Dandridge said, "is Alexander's older sister, Claire. In fact, I think you girls might go to the same middle school—Oakdale. Am I right?"

Unbelievable! My mouth dropped open. I know it did. And I don't blame Mrs. Dandridge for what happened next. She didn't know. It was not her fault.

(21) Claire

MELODY MATTERO? WHOA!

My heart did a somersault and landed in my throat! I didn't know what to do!

You could tell right off Melody knew who I was. The color drained from her face.

Her and me, we just stared at each other for a couple seconds—and then she came flying at me like a maniac! I remember hearing that woman, Mrs. Danderfield or whoever, hollering, "Melody! Melody! What's wrong?" Then that woman and my mother—both of them had to jump in to hold Melody off me.

"You liar!" Melody screamed.

"Stop, Melody! Stop!" that woman yelled.

But Melody was like a crazed animal! She lunged against everyone holding her back and managed to get in one good swipe. My hand stung, and I could see blood from where she scratched me.

"How could you do that? You liar!" Melody kept hollering.

Corky and Izzy started to cry, and other people came running. The gray horse Corky was supposed to ride threw his head back and skittered sideways, stepping on a woman's foot. When she yelled, the horse bolted.

It was a nightmare moment, and all I did was freeze up.

"Do you know what you've done to my dad?" Melody was still screaming while they dragged her off.

I was not going to deny it. No siree. I figured whatever she said, whatever she did, I deserved it.

After they hauled Melody into the little room with all the saddles and closed the door, things got quieter. Izzy and Corky were still crying, so Mom knelt down to scoop them into her arms. She looked up at me. "Claire? Are you okay?"

I hadn't moved. Not an inch. "I'm all right," I said in a flat voice.

Mom didn't seem to notice my *non*reaction.

"Let's get out of here," my mother said. "I had no idea who that girl was. No idea. She has been so wonderful to Corky. Oh, Claire, look at your hand, it's bleeding. Good Lord, I can't believe this."

Unbelievable was definitely the word. Of all the people in the world, Mr. Mattero's daughter had to be the one who worked with Corky at riding therapy? It was so random. I mean, what kind of fate is that?

I picked up the camera from where Mom had dropped it

and followed her back to the van where I helped buckle the kids in.

But all the way home, all evening, I felt terrible. All twisted up in knots inside. I kept reliving it, seeing how angry Melody was, hearing her scream. And here is the really weird thing: I suddenly realized that over the past several weeks I had repeated that stuff about what Mr. Mattero did so many times, it had become like the truth. And I don't think that during the whole time I ever once really stopped to think about what our lies had done to him, and to other people, like his family.

Mom tried to comfort me. Mom and Dad both. They had no idea what a low-life, cruddy liar I was, how it was all my fault.

I stayed in my room from the moment we got back from the stables. My mother washed off the little scratch on my hand and put some ointment on it. Then she brought me dinner on a tray, like I was sick, but I didn't touch it. She came in later with some pudding, which I could have eaten without even thinking about the calories because I hadn't eaten supper, but I didn't eat that either. I just let it sit there.

Later, after the kids were in bed, Mom came up again, to rub my back and tell me that the woman from the stables had called to apologize. She said they hoped Corky was okay and that he would return to riding therapy, to work with a new volunteer.

Not that I think my mom is stupid or anything, but did it ever once occur to either of my parents that maybe we had made up that story about what Mr. Mattero did? Their trust in me and all the things they did that night made me feel even worse. I wasn't comfortable being in my own skin.

At school the next day, we had a science test. It was the only thing anyone else talked or thought about all day. Except for me. Kids kept grilling each other. *"What are the four major types of air masses that affect the weather in the United States?"* *"What is atmosphere?"* *"What is convection?"* Who gave a crap? All I could think about was Melody Mattero, screaming. And my little sister and brother crying . . . *"What happens when a cold air mass meets a warm air mass?"* I knew the answer to that one! A storm. A raging, frickin' storm, which is what I had in my head!

After school everyone seemed giddy and glad the test was over. I guess I was the only one who didn't feel any relief.

I had my new bathing suit and stuff in a little sports bag. Half a peanut butter sandwich for an after-school snack because it was my day to try out the swim club gig. Phoebe had talked me into it. See? I was still trying to hold on to my new life while the old one kept sucking me under.

On the bus ride over to the pool, Phoebe and I sat with a group of girls that she knew. One of them passed out peanut M&M's. Another one of the girls asked me, "When you lived in North Carolina, Claire, did people talk with a southern accent?"

I hesitated because I didn't know, but I had to tell them something so I said, "Yeah, everyone down there talks with an accent." And the voice of Suzanne's older sister, Addy, echoed in my ears: *"The more you lie, the more you have to lie . . ."*

"How come *you* don't then?" another girl asked.

My chest got tight. I shrugged. "I don't know," I finally mumbled. But I don't think any of them thought about it much. I fidgeted with my watch. Pretty soon we were all talking about going to a movie at the mall on Saturday.

At the pool, Phoebe and I shared a locker. We jammed all our stuff in. Shoes and socks and jeans and all our underwear rolled into our shirts. She forced the locker door shut with her hip and locked it. Then, holding our bathing caps and towels, we picked our way over the wet tile through the shower area to the door that opened into the indoor pool.

The pool was already full of kids doing laps. A lifeguard's whistle blew and echoed in the massive building. We hugged our arms and shivered, it was so cold. Phoebe pointed to the lane where we'd swim, and after throwing our towels on a bench, we went to stand at the edge of the pool, our teeth chattering.

"Want me to go first?" Phoebe asked, loud because it was noisy.

I nodded vigorously.

She pulled her bathing cap on and stuffed all her long hair under it. Then she grinned at me and bravely dove in. Just like that! When her head resurfaced, she started doing a brisk crawl.

I took a deep breath, tucked my hair under that thin cap,

too, and reluctantly did the same, trying to make my dive, like, halfway respectable.

The water was a shock. I came up gulping for air. But it was amazing how quickly I got used to it. Up one lane, down another, I followed Phoebe's kicking feet. The exercise felt good, like it was making me breathe harder, but relaxing me inside, too. Briefly, there was a break from thinking about Melody Mattero. We did twenty laps before we stopped.

Pausing at the end of a lane, we rested our elbows on a narrow shelf while we caught our breath. Then we flipped our caps up just enough so we could hear each other.

"You're doing great!" Phoebe exclaimed.

I wiped the water out of my eyes. "I am?"

"Yes! I am so glad you came, Claire!"

"Me, too."

"I'm not kidding," Phoebe went on. "You are the best friend I've made at this school."

Why *then*? Why, why, why in the world did I choose that moment? I don't know, but I did. And this is what I said: "Yeah, and you're the best friend I have at this school, too, Phoebe, but I am not who you think I am."

Maybe I started to 'fess up because I didn't think I deserved a nice new friend like Phoebe after what I'd done.

Maybe because it had finally caught up with me.

Phoebe just smiled.

I figured maybe she didn't hear me.

"Phoebe," I repeated a little louder, inching my slippery hands along that wall toward Phoebe and the truth. "All that stuff I said? About me coming from North Carolina?"

Phoebe frowned a little. She bit the edge of her lip and tilted her head toward mine.

"It's not true. I made it up. I came from another middle school in the county—Oakdale—because two other girls and I told the principal we were abused by our music teacher."

Slowly, Phoebe nodded, in slow motion, like she understood everything. But how could she?

"Did you hear me?" I asked. Her reaction was, like, too good for me to believe.

"Yes, Claire. I know. I *heard* you. I *know* who you are."

"What?"

"I know who you are. The day before you came to our school, our English teacher talked about it. You know, because it was in the newspaper, and if kids found out who you were, she didn't want anyone giving you a hard time."

I couldn't believe it. "You *knew*?"

"It's okay."

"Does everyone at school know?"

Phoebe shook her head. "I don't think so. Just the kids in that class."

"Oh my gosh."

"Claire, it's all right. It doesn't matter."

Still, I was so bowled over by the news I turned away and

stared at the end of the pool. I stared so long my arms started to get cold.

"Yeah, but there's more," I finally said, turning back at Phoebe.

She ignored it and pushed off. "Come on! Ten more laps!" she yelled, her face disappearing beneath her arm, then all of her slipping beneath the water.

I pulled my cap down, but I remained treading water and watching with blurry eyes as Phoebe swam off. "Everything was a lie," I confessed out loud, even though no one but me could hear what I said.

Reluctantly, halfheartedly, I swam a little more. But after a few more laps, I told Phoebe I needed to quit. She said to unpin the locker key from her towel and go ahead in, so I did. I took a shower and got dressed and combed out my wet hair. Then, after discovering some change in my jeans pocket, I went to get a Diet Sprite while I waited for Phoebe to finish.

She was the last one out of the locker room and found me sitting at a small table near the snack machines. By then, everyone else had either left, or was waiting outside to be picked up by their parents.

I forced a smile when Phoebe walked in. "That was fun."

"You did great!" she said. "Have you already called your mom?"

I nodded. "I used the pay phone. She'll be here soon."

Phoebe dropped her backpack on one chair, then pulled out another and sat down. Her long hair was still wet. She rubbed it with a towel.

I wondered if I should finish what I had started saying in the pool, but I was scared.

Phoebe sensed I was uneasy. She glanced around like she was making sure no one was listening, then leaned forward, letting her hands and the wet towel rest in her lap. "Look, Claire," she said. "I meant it when I said it didn't matter to me what had happened to you. It doesn't mean that I don't care."

"Thanks," I told her. "I 'preciate it." I swallowed hard because I wanted to finish telling her the whole truth, but then what if she told someone else and Jenna found out? I leaned toward her. "But you don't understand," I began. "It's just that . . . see, I—"

"I *do* understand," Phoebe insisted.

I froze up, and, nervous, I started picking at a fingernail.

"Look at me, Claire," Phoebe said.

When I lifted my eyes, Phoebe reached across the table to touch my wrist. "I understand," she said, lowering her voice, "because it happened to me, too."

A cold feeling seized me. I stared at her.

"Yeah," she confirmed. Her eyes grew large and instantly became moist when she blinked. "By my stepfather." She pulled her hand back and wiped her lips. Her eyes fell away, then came back to find me sitting there—dumb and speechless. "It's still going on, too. Only I don't know how to stop it. I don't think my mom will believe me."

A tear spilled out of one of Phoebe's eyes and ran down her cheek.

"Oh, my God," I muttered.

"You're the only person I've told," Phoebe said. "'Cause you've been through it, Claire. So you know what it's like. It's one reason I wanted so bad to be your friend. Because, like, you'd understand."

Poor Phoebe, I thought. Her stepfather abusing her. I blinked and held my eyes closed briefly, not wanting to even imagine what that meant.

"This is serious—really serious, Phoebe," I said urgently. "You need to tell someone."

"No!" She shook her head vigorously and wiped away the tear with her fingers. "No way. I can't. My mom would kill me. And my stepfather would deny it. He said he would!"

Through the large glass windows, I saw my mother pulling up in our van.

I rolled my eyes. "My mom's here."

Phoebe pulled back. "It's okay."

"But I can't go *now*—"

"No really, it's okay. I'm getting picked up soon, too."

I started to stand up.

Phoebe folded her hands, like she was praying, and begged me, "Please don't tell anyone, Claire. Please don't."

"No, I won't tell," I feebly assured her.

I picked up my backpack and my duffel, and I started to walk away, then stopped and rushed back.

"Phoebe, will you be safe at home tonight? Do you want to come stay with me or something? I'm sure it would be okay with my mom."

She shook her head. "I'll be all right. Go ahead, Claire."

Still, I hesitated.

"*Go*, Claire. It's okay," she insisted.

So I left, but I knew Phoebe was not going to be okay. Not unless somebody spoke up for her.

When I walked out of the pool building, I stopped. The late-afternoon sun was warm. Two kids flew by on their Rollerblades, laughing. Mom waved to me from where she waited in the van across the street, and I could see Izzy sitting in her car seat in the back licking an ice-cream cone. Corky, beside her, had his arms crossed and was pouting. He was probably still angry about what had happened at the stables the day before. Already, he had stopped talking again. No telling when he would get over it. It could be weeks. And all because of me.

I closed my eyes and felt the tears rush in.

Because look at what I had done.

And look at what I knew.

I said to myself, that if I took another step, I had to tell the truth. I had to tell the truth about what Mr. Mattero did—which was nothing! And I had to tell someone about Phoebe so her stepfather wouldn't hurt her anymore. Even if it made her angry. Even if she never spoke to me again. Even if I had to go to yet *another* school.

"Claire, come on!" my mother called out the window.

I couldn't move. If I took a step, I had to tell.

Little white card. I thought of it, lying under my socks in the bureau drawer at home. It had Detective Daniels's number on it. *"My cell phone number's there, too. Call me anytime. Anytime at all."*

"Claire, what's wrong?" my mother yelled.

I squeezed my eyes shut even tighter. I was so afraid.

But if I took a step, I had to tell.

22 Melody

MRS. DANDRIDGE BROUGHT ME HOME from the stables the afternoon I tried to attack Claire Montague. Before I got out of the car she told me that no matter what Claire had done, it didn't give me the right to lash out. "I don't blame you for being angry, Melody," she said. "We all get angry. And I know these are extraordinary circumstances, but no one ever resolves anything by fighting."

I nodded. I told her she was right. I knew she was right. But I resented Mrs. Dandridge for being so reasonable. I vowed to myself that I would never ever return to the stables.

At home, I walked in and calmly told my family what had just happened.

Cade was impressed. "All *right!*" he cheered, trying to give me a high five. I thought I detected the trace of a smile on Mom, too, although she averted her face quickly and didn't say anything, just asked me to help her set the table.

Dad opened his arms to me. But I didn't want to hug Dad. I

pretended I didn't see his outstretched arms and rushed out of the room, saying I needed to take a shower.

The next day I stayed home from school again because Mom thought I should have a day to cool off. I arranged for Liz to bring me a book I needed, as well as homework assignments. But it was Annie who knocked on our door.

I was surprised.

"May I come in?" Annie asked.

I hesitated, but I opened the door all the way for her.

Annie stepped into our front hall and handed me my grammar book with its bright green smiley-face cover. "Your homework's in there. It's in the book."

I saw the assignment sheets sticking out of the pages.

"Thanks," I said.

"Melody, look," Annie said. "Whatever happens, I just want you to know how sorry I am for not going to your house that night, and for my parents. For them not letting me go—and then not answering the door when your dad knocked on it. They were wrong. It's just that they were scared."

"Of what?" I asked.

Annie shook her head. "I don't know. None of us knows. But we feel bad about it. We're really sorry, Mel."

I sucked in my breath. If her parents were sorry, then why weren't they here apologizing, too? We caught each other's eyes, looked away again.

"Look, I won't stay," Annie said. "I just wanted to tell you that."

I fumbled with the book in my hands, bit my lip, looked at Annie, and then looked down. I was still disappointed in her. But I was glad she had come, too.

Annie left, and softly I closed the door. But I watched from the long, narrow window in the foyer as she walked down the sidewalk to her mother's car. And I kept watching, even as they drove away.

Odd how things happen. Another five minutes, and Annie would have been there when the police pulled up.

Each time Detective Daniels had come to see us previously he was in an unmarked car. But this time it was a regular cruiser. So I wondered if this was it. Was this the moment they would arrest my father and take him to jail?

Suddenly, in a panic, I rushed out the back door to get Mom, who was pulling at the Virginia creeper in the ivy. "Mom, the police are here!"

She dropped a handful of vines on the lawn, and we walked back in quickly, Mom taking off her garden gloves and brushing at the loose dirt on her jeans.

At the front door, we could see Detective Daniels coming up the walk. Mom opened the door before he even had a chance to knock. Right away, he saw the scared look on my mother's face.

"Relax," he said, holding up a hand as though to stop us. "I've actually come with some good news this time."

Mom, still clutching her garden gloves, put a hand on her heart.

"You did? You came with good news?" I asked.

"Yes." He smiled at us both. "Is Fred here?"

Mom seemed paralyzed, so he turned to me. "Melody, is your dad home?"

"Yes—I'll go get him," I offered, rushing off while Mom led Detective Daniels into our living room .

When Dad, Cade, Mom, and I were all seated in the living room, Detective Daniels rubbed his hands together and nodded at my father. "You're off the hook, Fred. One of the girls confessed. A second one confirmed it. We haven't gotten in touch with the third one yet, she's living out-of-state now, but there's no doubt in my mind she'll change her story after she's heard what the other two had to say."

"Dad, that's great!" I exclaimed, jumping out of my seat.

Mom put one hand over her mouth and the other on Dad's shoulder.

My father seemed stunned. He took in a big breath. "Finally," is all he said.

"What happened? What did the girl say?" Mom wanted to know.

"Was it Claire?" I asked, sitting back down.

"Yes, it was Claire," Detective Daniels confirmed. "How did you know?"

Mom, Dad, Cade, and I glanced at one another and smirked.

"Mellie almost tackled her yesterday," Cade said.

Detective Daniels raised his eyebrows at me.

"But I didn't hurt her or anything!"

"Well, who knows?" he said. "Maybe that was the turning point. Although there were other things, too, that came out. Something involving yet another girl." He didn't elaborate on that, but he did fill us in on all the sordid details of the girls' conspiracy, how they plotted to tell the lie just to get out of Dad's class and how Jenna thought the attention might bring her mother back, even though she never told the other girls that it was part of her motivation.

"Then it sounds as though two of them just went along with the lie to get out of Fred's class," Mom reiterated. "But *why*?"

"Bored? Who knows? In their eyes, it was a friendship thing," Detective Daniels replied. "They figured they'd get a study hall instead of music."

"That's it?" Mom asked, incredulous. "They were bored?"

Detective Daniels shrugged. "Sometimes that's all it is."

My mother covered her eyes.

"Claire is a very sad and contrite young lady," he went on. "She didn't realize how much their lie would hurt so many people."

"But why did it take her so long to say something?" I asked

him. "I mean, she saw me at school every day. She had to know how much we were hurting!"

Detective Daniels disagreed. "I'm not sure she realized that, Melody. Kids that age—even your age, sometimes they don't look much beyond themselves. I'm no psychiatrist, but from my own experience I can tell you this: some of them just enjoy being the center of attention and the reason for all the fuss."

"But for all those weeks?" I still didn't understand.

"Well, once they lie they feel they have to stick with it or else risk getting into even bigger trouble," he tried to explain. "Eventually, if they have a conscience, it'll bother them—or one of them. All it takes is one. That's why we kept going back to these girls, interviewing them again and again to see if there were any discrepancies in their stories. Especially in a case like this, where your dad passed the lie-detector test."

"You make it sound as though this happens all the time," Mom said. She was holding Dad's hand.

"Too often, if you ask me," the detective replied. "One in five cases of alleged sexual abuse in our county turns out to be false."

We were all quiet for a moment.

"What happens now?" Dad asked.

"From here I go to Oakdale," Detective Daniels said. "I'm sure they'll be in touch, but I assume you can go back to work immediately.

"As for the girls," he continued, "we'll file charges against

them for making false statements to police. They'll go to juvenile court and most likely have to perform some community
service. They may be kept on some sort of home detention for
a while, too, where they can't talk on the phone or be with
friends during the week. I can't be sure, but the judge may even
order them to sit in a jail cell for the afternoon, just so they
know what it's like. So they know where they almost put you,
Fred."

Less than an hour later, Mrs. Fernandez sat in our living room,
urging Dad to return to school on Monday, telling him how
much he had been missed, how eager she was to have the band
practicing again.

Dad's stunning answer was loud and clear: "Thanks, Helena,"
he said. "But I won't be returning to Oakdale."

Mrs. Fernandez wouldn't accept it. "Fred, you have to come
back! You're a great teacher! You can't let these girls destroy
your career!"

Dad almost laughed. "Well, they pretty much took care of
that. Any trust I had in those kids is gone."

"Fred, *please*. Think this over. Promise me you will take a few
days to think this over."

Dad did not respond.

Mrs. Fernandez sighed. "I feel as though this is my fault. That
all of us in the school system bend over backward to educate
these kids about what kind of touching is appropriate, and

what's not. We *encourage* them to come forward if they suspect something is not right . . . and yet look what happens."

My principal looked at us sadly. "Sometimes they don't think through the consequences, you know? They're kids—" She held her hands palm up. "And sometimes they're just plain . . . goofy."

Mom nodded, but her lips were pressed together, and neither she nor Dad said anything.

"Try to talk some sense into him, Mary," Mrs. Fernandez begged my mother as the three of us walked back to the front door. "We need teachers like Fred."

"I have to leave that decision to my husband," Mom replied. She put her arm around my shoulders. "You have no idea what he's been through these past several weeks. No matter how many apologies there are now, there is no changing what happened. No going back in time. He's different now. We all are.

"And I'm not sure," Mom told her, "that we can ever put back what those girls took away."

23 Claire

AT FIRST, THEY DIDN'T BELIEVE ME.

"You lied about Mr. Mattero, Claire. Surely you can under-stand why we're a little doubtful about *this*." Detective Daniels looked me in the eye when he said that, and I didn't blink. Afterward, he took careful notes. And I spelled Phoebe's name for him.

"You have to do something right now," I urged him, "because Phoebe may not even be safe tonight. You've got to believe me! Part of the whole reason why I am telling you the truth is that I want someone to help her."

"We will," he assured me. "We will send someone right away."

"Thank you," I said, and a funny noise came out of my throat. I cried a little. I guess because all that time had gone by, and I didn't realize what a bad thing we'd done and how much I'd hurt the Matteros—and my own family, too.

Poor Mom. She started crying, too. And after she'd been so good about it, like when I first told her we needed to talk.

I had waited until we got home from the pool, until Corky and Izzy had eaten and were in bed, before I said anything to her. Finally, when Mom and I were alone in the kitchen, after we got the dishwasher going, I said to her in a pretty calm voice: "Mom, you need to take me down to the police station. Either that, or you need to let me invite that detective to our house because there is something really important I have to tell him *and* you and Dad."

Her eyes got big. "Claire, what are you saying?"

"I'm saying I need to talk to Detective Daniels. And to you and Dad." I handed her the little white card with the detective's phone number on it.

I worried that maybe Mom thought it was something else— like maybe she thought Mr. Mattero had abused us even worse but I'd never had the guts to tell her. She looked scared, but she knew it was important. I don't know, since I changed schools we'd been able to talk more to each other. All that time driving home from Decker, maybe—plus she liked Phoebe. Whatever it was, she didn't get hysterical on me the way she might have before. Instead, she put a hand up near her throat, but she went right over to the phone and called Detective Daniels.

Thank goodness he was at the police station that night. He said he'd be right over. He drove up at almost the same time as my father.

After we were all sitting down at the kitchen table, my parents on either side of me, I took a breath and told them straight out. I said, "What Mr. Mattero did, what we said he did? It was all a lie."

Mom gasped.

"What?" Dad cried.

Detective Daniels handed me a pad of lined paper. He asked me to write it down for him, and I did.

> What we said Mr. Mattero did was a lie.
>
> Mr. Mattero did not give Jenna a hug.
>
> Mr. Mattero did not put his arms around me and pat me on the butt.
>
> Mr. Mattero did not try to hug Suzanne. He did not rub his hand up and down her back.

After I finished and handed the paper to Detective Daniels, Dad pushed his chair back and looked at me. "Why?" he asked. "Why did you girls do this, Claire?"

I shrugged. "'Cause Jenna asked us to."

On the other side of me, Mom sat quietly. She had stopped crying.

"Because Jenna asked you to," Dad repeated.

I couldn't look at him. I stared into my lap. "We were friends, and she asked us to do it. Plus, we just kind of wanted to get out of Mr. Mattero's class because it was kind of slow and none of us was into music all that much."

"It had to have been more than that," Mom insisted. I could

feel her staring at me. "Jenna was up to something, wasn't she, Claire?"

I shook my head. "No. I mean, yeah, it was Jenna's idea and all that. And I guess she wanted to get back at her mom, or get her mom's attention or something—because her mom was seeing that other guy. But we didn't even know that stuff about Jenna's mom in the beginning. Mainly we did it because she asked us to and we were friends. Suzanne and me and Jenna— we three didn't have any other friends at Oakdale. We never thought it was going to hurt a whole bunch of people."

I never saw Phoebe again. She was in and out of my life, just like that. She wasn't at school the next day, or the next week. Finally, I heard from another friend of hers that Phoebe's mother had taken her out of school because they had to move back to Kentucky for an emergency. Mom called Detective Daniels to find out if that was true, and he confirmed it. He told us that Phoebe and her family had moved. But her stepfather did not go with them.

The kids in the swim club don't know what happened to Phoebe. They thought it was really weird the way she disappeared. "What kind of family emergency?" they kept asking. On the bus, on the way to swim practice, while we ate peanut M&M's, I was tempted to make up something to cover for her, but I caught myself. What I said was, "Sometimes people have to move right away and there isn't even time for good-bye."

———

I know that we'll be punished, Suzanne and me—and Jenna, too, even if she is in a different state. But I'm ready. Nothing that happens from here on out can be worse than what I've already been through. Hiding the lie was a lot worse than coming forward and telling the truth, I'll tell you that.

Plus, the whole thing has made me appreciate my family. We definitely talk more, especially my mom and me, even if it's just while we're making dinner or, like I said, in the van coming home from the pool with Corky and Izzy asleep in the backseat.

I love my parents for not holding what I did against me. That's not to say they weren't mad at me for what I did! No way. I spent a lot of time alone, in my room, but it made me smarten up. I mean, I'm definitely starting to eat normally because not only do I feel better, but I can think better, too! I'm swimming—and this is actually funny, my finger got better from all the chlorine.

I don't know, I am who I am, and there are kids at Decker who actually want to be my friends. Although I guess we'll see what happens to that after I go to juvenile court . . .

Suzanne and I aren't allowed to see each other right now. But I hope she feels relieved, the same as me. I will always remember that it was Suzanne who really didn't want to lie in the first place. It didn't feel right, she kept saying. Man, I wished I'd listened.

I wrote a letter to Mr. Mattero and to Melody, too. I told them how sorry I was that they had suffered. I asked Melody to please reconsider being a volunteer at the horse barns. But I know that letter wasn't enough. How could it be?

"It's over now," Mom keeps telling me. "Put it behind you and get on with your life, Claire."

"Yeah, it's over," I agree and tell myself. "It's over." Maybe if I say it enough times I'll believe it.

On the other hand, maybe I finally learned to recognize what's right and what's wrong, and so maybe I'm smart enough now to know that it will never be over. Because what Jenna, Suzanne, and I did in the seventh grade at Oakdale will always be part of who we are, and who we become.

It's really weird, but sometimes I can step back from it and, like, look into the future and actually feel a little bit good about it. Am I a totally heartless, evil person to say that? No, I don't think so. It's just that if none of this happened, well, for one thing, no one would have ever known about Phoebe.

Plus, besides that, it has, like, changed me into a different person. A person who will never be pushed around again by someone like Jenna. A person who knows it's not who you hang out with, or how skinny you are, or how you do your eyes that matters, it's who you are inside. I made a mistake, yes, but because of it, hopefully, I'm a little bit better person.

To thine own self be true. I don't ever want to be uncomfortable in my own skin again.

And *that* is the honest truth. Totally.

(24) Melody

I REALLY WANTED DAD to return to teaching, to show every-body how those girls didn't ruin his life. But he wouldn't. He wouldn't go back to Oakdale Middle School. Mom got him a job at the nursery instead, where he heads up a landscape crew. He drives a red pickup truck and works with three His-panic men delivering mulch, mowing lawns, trimming bushes, and fixing sprinkler systems. He says he enjoys being outside all the time, and he likes his coworkers. Dad's teaching them English, and they're teaching him Spanish. They keep telling Dad how lucky he is, to live in a country of so much opportu-nity and wealth—and freedom of speech.

It embarrassed me—it made me angry—that Dad did not go back to school. He isn't making half the money he made as a teacher. Mom is even talking about getting a second job. But the worst thing was how Dad wasn't the same anymore, not even at home. Something inside of him died.

I couldn't even ask my father about the annual canoe trip. Three whole days with just Dad? I wasn't sure what we'd talk about.

Mom has said all along we shouldn't tell Song about all this until the end of summer because she would feel bad the whole time she was away at camp in Maine, where she'd been hired as a counselor. A lot of people, not just my sister, have no idea what happened to Dad. What happened to *us*. If you don't read the local newspaper or have kids at Oakdale, how would you know? We kept it quiet to save Dad the embarrassment, but even that makes me angry, because it's like Dad was forced to live a secret life for a crime he didn't commit!

It seemed so unfair that those girls—Jenna, Suzanne, and Claire—were never publicly shamed the way my dad was. They remained "unidentified" in the local newspaper because they're "minors."

It didn't stop either . . . we went to my brother's end-of-the-year sports banquet at the high school, and while we were standing in line, waiting to get a soda, one of Cade's coaches came over to Dad and shook his hand. "It's good to see you, Fred," he said, clapping Dad on the shoulder. "I hope things are going well." But he didn't stay to chitchat for long, and when he walked away, I saw him glance back over his shoulder. I wondered what he was thinking because I'd overheard Mom and Dad talking one night about how they feared people were still suspicious. *Three girls? Telling the same story? Sticking to it for so long? There had to be something going on there.*

This is what we can't change. We can't change the way people think, the way people look at us. And don't say it doesn't matter because it does matter. That's the most frustrating thing. It's what those lies left us. Our legacy, Mom has said. I tried writing a poem about it once, but I only got as far as the title. So the title just sits there, at the top of an empty sheet of lined paper in my journal—"The Legacy of a Lie"—waiting for me to delicately pick the words from my aching, bruised heart.

A month went by, and summer came. Dad finally agreed to talk with a family counselor. And after all the phone calls from Mrs. Dandridge and that letter from Claire, I promised Mom I would reconsider going back to the barns. I missed the horses, yes, but mostly, I missed the kids.

Cade left for football camp in North Carolina. But when Song came home to unload all her boxes from college and start packing for her camp job, I sat on her bed and told her what had happened. I didn't do it to hurt her. I didn't do it to make her feel guilty and cry. I did it because I figured she was part of the family. I did it because I needed her. And I needed her to know.

"Why didn't you tell me?" she asked, throwing up her arms. "All this time! Come on! What's with you guys?" She was pretty upset we'd kept her in the dark. After stomping around her room and throwing a couple things around, she sat on the bed with me.

"I'll bet it makes you think twice about becoming a teacher," I said, smoothing out a section of her bedspread in front of me.

We were sitting cross-legged, facing each other, and although I didn't lift my eyes, I could tell my sister had folded her arms and was looking at me. "Think twice about it?" she repeated my question. "Maybe. But it doesn't make me want to give up the idea of teaching."

I looked up at her, surprised.

Song took my hands. "I think that's part of the challenge, Mel. Kids making mistakes and helping them figure things out."

I may have rolled my eyes, I'm not sure.

"Look, I *know* how much this hurt," Song went on. "It kills me to think about it. But it's all about forgiveness. You and Mom and Dad—Cade, too—you all need to let go of what happened or it'll eat up all the space in your hearts. There won't be room for anything else."

I thought about what my sister said. I thought about it a lot. I don't know how she got so smart, but I think she's right. In the end, it's all about us, finding it in ourselves to forgive those three girls for what they did. It's all about us, forgiving the people at school—and everywhere else—who *still* don't understand. It's all about me, forgiving my best friend, Annie, and her parents for being afraid. And maybe toughest of all, it's all about me forgiving Dad for getting drunk that night and respecting his decision not to return to teaching.

One thing about Song: she doesn't just say something and walk away. She needled all of us until she left. She got me and Annie together and took us to a movie and for ice cream, and I came home knowing Annie and I could still be friends, even if the friendship was a little different. Then Song fixed dinner for our family one night—black beans and rice and fruit salad because she's a vegetarian now—and she actually made my parents laugh.

"Don't be so hard on yourself," Song whispered into my ear before she drove off with a friend to Maine to begin work.

So I'm trying. I gave Dad a new box of clarinet reeds for Father's Day. And I asked him, "Do you think maybe we could schedule that canoe trip?"

He grinned, and I thought his eyes got shiny. "Let's do it in July before the water gets too low," he said.

I keep thinking that it's a little like my mother struggling to yank out all that Virginia creeper in the garden. The weed is so stubborn that Mom has to pull with everything she has—and sometimes, when it finally lets go, she falls backward. But she's kept at it and, little by little, her efforts have made a difference. There's still a lot left. But now, in all the places where the weed's been pulled, the ivy is thriving.

Acknowledgments

I wish to acknowledge and warmly thank the following people: Christina Koch and Jennifer Lee of the Anne Arundel County Department of Social Services; Detective Dan Long, Anne Arundel County Police Child-Abuse Unit; Diane Finch, Head of Guidance, Anne Arundel County Public Schools; Catherine Shultz, Phyllis Crossen-Richardson, Maryland Therapeutic Riding, and Indian Creek Middle School, especially Anne Chambers (head) and teachers Greg Bush and Brad Woodward.